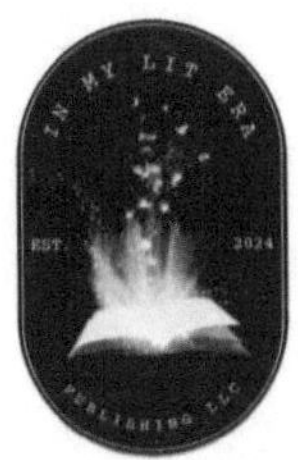

First published by In My Lit Era Publishing LLC 2025

First edition

EPUB ISBN: 978-1-965557-04-4

PAPERBACK ISBN: 978-1-965557-05-1

Cover art by Stacey LP

Typeset and formatted by Stacey LP

Copy and Line Editing by Sam Willow of Scrollwork Edits

BETWEEN THE LINES

AN AFTERGLOW RISING NOVELLA

AFTERGLOW RISING TRILOGY
BOOK 2.5

STACEY LP

COMMITMENT TO DIVERSE
WORLDS IN SCI-FI AND FANTASY

Why is diversity important? Because *people* are diverse in experience, appearance, beliefs, sexuality, gender identity, and so much more. That is why I strive to include an array of characters in my work who represent the intersectionality of our real world.

As a bisexual female author, I know that representation is essential for readers to connect with and see themselves across all genres. And what better genre to embrace diversity than science fiction and fantasy—where new worlds can be anything we want them to be? Because leaders, heroes, and love come in many forms.

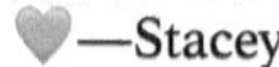—Stacey

CONTENT AWARENESS

The *Afterglow Rising Trilogy* takes place in a post-apocalyptic setting and gets quite stressful. You can expect strong language/cursing throughout the text.

Happy endings are not guaranteed.

Content:

• Aliens

• Medical procedures

• Abduction

• Eight-legged creatures

• Violence

• Depictions of anxiety, panic attacks

• References to and experience of loss and death

• Cult-like depictions

• Open-door love scenes (eventually...)

I apologize in advance for the myriad of emotions you are about to experience throughout this trilogy. Kind of.

Okay have fun, bye!

To Loren Lee,
For listening to all of my unhinged out of context ramblings, and talking me down from all the spirals.

SEPTEMBER 1, 2025

I'D ALWAYS EXPECTED the apocalypse to be triggered by nuclear war, some kind of viral pandemic, or a catastrophic climate event.

One kill switch.

Bam!

The end.

But the beginning of the end had been quiet. A breath held in, waiting for release.

Today didn't feel much different.

As our truck crept down the driveway, I squeezed my eyes shut, trying to keep the telltale burn of tears at bay. My greatest fears had sprung to life as I'd slept, and I couldn't help thinking there was more I could have done to prevent it.

Waking up to screaming, the gut punch of loss, the silence of our group as we'd struggled to connect, knowing that nothing would be the same—again. I had voted for the path that had led us here, cursed by my perpetual idealistic hope. I'd *fought* for it when I should have just listened.

As our truck slowed to turn at the bottom of the drive, I looked back at Carter and Jason, still standing where we'd left them. Uncertainty was a crushing weight, and it was getting harder to fight the pressure to give in. As I struggled to push my doubts back down beneath the surface, still, I promised—

I won't give up.

I won't forget.

When we come back together, I'll never say goodbye again.

My eyes blinked open as our car groaned to a stop. The sun was high in the sky, but the cool air blowing from the AC kept the late afternoon heat at bay. When we'd stopped at the last parking lot, we'd jumpstarted the SUV I was riding in now. Relief didn't even begin to describe how I'd felt when I'd finally settled into the back seat of our second car after riding in the rear of our truck all morning. The gas tank had been nearly full, too. Talk about luck.

I took off my glasses to rub the sleep from my eyes, cringing as a sharp twinge pinched in my neck. Putting them back on, I glanced in the car's rearview mirror. Light stubble lined my dark tan jawline, and my short black hair was sticking up in every direction. I could see the bags under my almond-shaped brown eyes from here— another tell-tale sign of the exhaustion from the past, well, almost year now.

"Ugh, how long was I asleep?" I mumbled, rubbing the knots from my stiff muscles as I lifted my head from where I was leaning against Dan's shoulder.

Deep circles underneath his dark brown eyes hinted at the depths of his exhaustion, and he fought off a yawn as he stretched his arms over his head. "Really Brian? You passed out about five minutes into our drive. Deadass, you were sleeping so hard, I was starting to think that this was just my life now."

"Would that really be so bad of a life?" I joked half-heartedly, raising an eyebrow.

Dan snorted a laugh, and I couldn't help the smile that pulled at the corner of my mouth in response.

Sam yawned from the front passenger seat where she sat beside

Russell, who was driving. "Destined to be in a cuddle puddle with Brian? I mean, there are worse occupations"

"I could totally vibe with that." Russell shot a crooked smile my way in the rearview mirror. "Where do I apply?"

"Y'all are ridiculous." Dan rolled his eyes, pushing open the door.

We were all trying to pretend things were normal. And in moments like these with my closest friends, it almost felt real. The four of us—the Twenty-Somethings, as our group called us, had built such a close bond since joining our camp. We hadn't known each other before the invasion, but now these people were everything to me.

I'd been visiting a few people on UT Campus when the alien ship appeared in Austin's sky. I was supposed to meet up with my friends before seeing a guest lecturer together, but the shelter-in-place order hit first. By the time I realized the order wasn't going to end, my friends had already left.

Without me.

Once everyone started running, all bets were off. Every second of every day was just trying to make it long enough to see the next sunrise. So quickly, the invaders had stolen our lives, forcing us into a near constant state of fight-or-flight. We all had stories of who we were before, of the places that had led us to each other. Each step shaped the path of our survival.

Even with so many unknowns, there was one thing I knew for sure. The friends I'd found in this group—we were always destined to come together. They were what kept me moving forward.

As we stepped out of the SUV into the bright sun, I hung back, taking a deep breath. We still hadn't talked about what our next moves were and I was sure I wasn't the only one dreading the conversation.

An alien-worshipping cult, The Community, had kidnapped Alina the night before while we had all been sleeping. Carter and Jason had taken off on what seemed like a suicide mission into the hellscape that our world had become in order to find her. And now, here we were, trying to uncover a way forward that would allow us to save the people we cared about as the pull of uncertainty clung to our heels. Every day brought new risks that threatened to take away the people I loved—and I had no idea how we could possibly begin to fix any of it.

The depths of heartache from reliving each event were ever-present, threatening to pull me under. And I was beyond tired from perpetually treading water, trying to stay afloat.

As we formed a circle next to the truck, my attention was immediately drawn to Emma, who was staring at a patch of grass at her feet. Emma had been with Alina earlier that morning, and had been knocked unconscious just before Alina had been taken. The bright blue of her irises contrasted the deep purple bruise framing her eye. Though Dan and Michelle protectively stood at her side, she made no move to acknowledge their presence, her expression blank and unchanging.

For more than eight months, Emma had thought that her brother, Jason, and her best friend, Alina, were gone for good. She had mourned them and come to terms with the fact that she might never see the two people she loved most in the world, again. She'd built nearly impenetrable walls to keep everyone else from getting too close, even switching to a nickname, Red, instead of her real name. She'd said that since she changed groups so frequently, the nickname was easier for new people to remember. The unspoken truth was that it was also a way for her to distance herself further from the life she'd lost.

We stood there in silence as the weight of the day's events settled heavily around us in the midday heat. Finally, Cap took a deep breath, preparing to address the group.

"We have a lot to figure out. At this point we should be far enough from where we dropped the tracker that we can safely take a break and make plans for what to do next."

As Cap spoke, my eyes darted to Gabriela, who shifted uncomfortably at the mention of the tracker that had been extracted from the wound on the back of her neck. Gabriela had been held captive by The Community since she'd escaped the alien medical labs where she'd been kept in some kind of incubation pod. We still didn't know the extent of what the invaders had done to her. The only evidence left behind from the experiments was a bright blue tattoo that ran down the length of her back and glowed when she was scared, which was almost constantly at this point. Sander's hand slipped around hers, the act of comfort likely just as much for him as it was for his friend.

From what he'd told us about The Community, if he and Gabriela were recaptured, even his status as Willa's little brother wouldn't be enough to protect him from the repercussions. He'd explained how his sister had been part of the Sovereign Council of The Community, the governing body in charge. Though, we all knew now that the doctor we'd only heard about secondhand—Dr. Don—was really at the head of it all.

Though Sander might have been Sovereign by association, by leaving, he'd become a traitor. He'd risked everything to free Gabriela from the tests she'd endured at the doctor's hands, sympathizing with the girl who was being held captive in his home. The punishment for that kind of treason—interfering with the doctor's plans—was death.

"I know we're all shaken from everything that's happened over the last twenty-four hours, but we can't let our emotions dictate our actions," Cap continued. "We're going to need to carefully think about what we need to do next, and how to make it happen."

"We should go back," Sam interrupted, voice breaking. Her eyes widened in surprise, like she hadn't meant to say the words out loud. She tilted her head back, pushing her thick curly hair over her shoulders as she slowly let out a shaky breath. As she made eye contact with Cap again, she continued, "Leaving them was a mistake. Carter and Jason can't take on The Community alone. They'll be in just as much danger as Alina. They need us."

Cap opened their mouth, but no words came out. Instead, their shoulders dropped in resignation. Seeing our usually fearless leader at a loss for words only made our situation that much more real.

Aside from their partner, Michelle, Carter was the person Cap had been closest to. They'd leaned on him just as much as Carter had looked up to them. It was clear that they were struggling coming to terms balancing the logic that protected our group with the heartache the decision had brought.

The silence dragged on. Clearly, no one knew what to say.

Finally Michelle picked up the discussion, taking the lead. "Carter and Jason made a choice. So did we. It might not feel right. I know it hurts. But I do believe that we've made the best decision we could. We have to trust that they'll find a way to take care of themselves until we can round up enough backup to help them get Alina *and* the others out—until we *know* we can survive the fight."

"So we're just going to let them go, even though they might not survive?" Sam glared. "How is that right?"

"It isn't too late. We can probably catch up to them, right?" Russell added, almost hesitantly. I could tell by the look on his face, he still wasn't sure about our decision, either.

I wanted to weigh in, but I couldn't find the words. Hell, I wanted to go back, too. I hated the idea of Carter and Jason out there alone. Their supplies were low, and if the rattling engine in the truck we'd left them with was any indication, I'd be surprised if they made it more than thirty miles before the rust bucket crapped out. Neither of them were thinking straight, which meant they'd be more likely to make mistakes, act on impulse. It was a recipe for disaster and we'd just abandoned them to deal with the fallout alone.

But if we'd stayed at the abandoned farm any longer to deliberate whether to let Carter and Jason go off alone, it would have only given The Community more opportunity to track us down again. We wanted Alina back, but we needed help. And who knew how long it would take to find reinforcements, let alone convince them that the fight was worth having?

In the end, we'd had to leave, and they hadn't wanted to come with us.

"I don't know why we are still having this conversation," Emma finally said, eyes cold as stone. I held my breath, waiting for the anger, the argument. But her voice remained desolate, empty with defeat. "The decision's made. They left. We're moving forward. End of story."

Sam's lips parted as if she was going to fight back, but after another moment she just nodded, resigned to Emma's statement.

Cap cleared their throat, their jaw tense. "We'll start with the property here, and if it's safe, we'll set up camp inside. Now that we know we hopefully aren't being tracked, we need to clear our heads and come up with a real plan before we make another move."

The house we'd stopped at was isolated enough, miles from the nearest neighborhoods. It was never a given that the place would truly be vacant. But there were signs. Fallen branches, likely from earlier spring storms, blocked the doors to the house, which indicated no one had been there in a while—we'd have to clear them in order to get inside. No windows were broken, or even cracked open. All of which pointed to the fact that no one had entered or left this house recently.

By the time we were ready to call for volunteers to search the house, I was the first to raise my hand. I could use the distraction and I wanted to feel useful. Russell and Dan volunteered as well, but in the end Dan and I were chosen to go together. Cap handed me a walkie-talkie, then Dan and I silently moved toward the house.

We carefully stepped through the tall grass. Thanks to the invaders, Texas wildlife was flourishing from the lack of humans intruding on their space. Sometimes it was hard to remember amidst the attacks from giant, blue-striped, eight-legged hell-creatures that there were still regular dangers to be wary of. And in this economy? The last thing we needed was a rattlesnake bite.

As we circled the house, we discovered a downed tree blocking the back door, and the windows were smudged with dirt and dust, obscuring our view of the inside. We worked quietly, moving enough of the brush away from the front door so that we'd be able to get it open.

"Ready, B?" Dan asked, studying me as we paused.

It was no different from how we'd begun each of our explorations, but the words held extra meaning today. Were we ready to keep moving forward after leaving so much behind?

"Always," I lied, forcing what I hoped sounded like confidence. "I'll go first."

As I moved to open the door, Dan held out an arm, blocking my path. He stepped in front of me with a half smile. "Nah, man. Not with your heavy feet. Let me go."

He entered the house and paused, listening, then signaled for me to follow. We left the door open to start airing the place out, as well as to create a clear path for escape if we needed to, as we scanned for any sign of life inside. My heart pounded as I shifted to stand back-to-back with Dan so we could keep eyes on the whole room, nerves buzzing underneath my skin.

Dan's arm pressed against mine, and the comforting warmth reminded me that I wasn't alone. He was still right there beside me. Together, we could do this.

The house was a split-level with a decent amount of ground to cover. The furniture, pictures, and belongings that were casually scattered around left the home in a kind of stasis—a snapshot of a day in the life. I always liked studying the items left behind, not just to decide what was useful, but to get an idea of what the previous occupants had been like.

Family portraits lined the walls: a man, two little boys, and a young girl. Toys and books scattered across the floor like a minefield, in what I imagined was probably just one day's worth of mess. I couldn't help wondering where they were now.

As we moved deeper into the house, I pulled at the collar of my shirt to try and fan some air against my sweaty skin. We weren't doing much more than creeping around, but the stale heat was stifling from being locked inside with no airflow.

School papers lay scattered across the kitchen table. Everything was casually placed—messy, but not harried. No sign of struggle was always a relief. At least then I could imagine that the family who had lived here before had been able to evacuate safely. Maybe they were even still out there somewhere.

"Upstairs next?" Dan spoke low, and I jumped.

"Geeze, you're too damn quiet," I whispered back, heart pounding.

A light sheen of sweat covered his dark brown skin, and his eyes shone with amusement as he smirked. "That's the *damn* point, B. Take notes."

I suppressed a chuckle as he patted my shoulder, a reassuring touch as he slipped past me and back down the hallway.

Everything always seemed easier when it was just Dan and me.

Before we'd met the others, we'd both been part of another group. We'd looked out for each other, supported one another, and made it through the roughest points of the invasion together. Dan had become my best friend—my person. As long as I could look over and see him by my side, I could always figure out a way to get through the rest.

Just as we reached the staircase, Dan abruptly stopped. His arm shot back and he grabbed my wrist, squeezing once—a warning.

I held my breath, forcing myself to ignore the ache in my ribs as I held the oxygen in my lungs. The house was so still, and for a few seconds I didn't hear anything.

Then, the slight sound of skittering and scratching above our heads sent a chill down my spine. My blood froze as my eyes slowly lifted toward the ceiling, half expecting to see a hell-creature stalking us from above, ready to drop down and devour us whole. But all I saw was a faint crack spiderwebbing across the ceiling.

A bead of sweat trickled down my neck, but I didn't dare move to brush it away. Not until we figured out where the sound was coming from. My pulse raced in anticipation of an attack and it took another moment before I could push the fear down far enough to focus.

The scratching was light, delicate—like a small animal. I released my breath slowly, the squeeze in my ribs subsiding ever so slightly.

Dan's shoulders relaxed as he likely came to the same conclusion. He peered over his shoulder, catching my eye, and the corner of his mouth tilted up as he whispered, "Squirrel, raccoon, or possum?"

"As long as it isn't a murder-pig," I responded in a hushed tone.

Dan breathed a quiet, amused laugh before turning back around. He kept his hand loosely wrapped around my wrist, still cautious, making sure I was close as we crept up the stairs. Was it necessary? Probably not. But I wasn't about to say anything in protest.

At the top of the stairs, two hallways stretched in opposite directions, and a bathroom stood directly in front of us with the door wide open. It was strangely reminiscent of the house we'd been staying in around the time Carter and I had found Alina and Jason. As I thought about them, the ache in my chest returned, pulsing with each beat of my heart. So much for finding distraction in routine.

"What's wrong?" Dan picked up on the change immediately, dropping my arm as he shot a look down each hallway to make sure we were still alone.

"Nothing—let's just finish up," I whispered back.

No sooner had I spoken the words, the mysterious skittering creature darted between us. Dan let out a startled yelp, scrambling to make space, and I nearly tripped over my own feet as the long-tailed, gray, fuzzy creature raced down the stairs.

I barely held in a relieved laugh. "It's just a rat."

Dan grimaced as the rodent raced out of sight. "No. Nope. We're not staying here."

I blinked, taken aback. After all of the wildlife we'd come across, I'd take a chonky old rat over most of the other creatures we'd encountered. "What? Why not? Rats are cool!"

Dan adamantly shook his head. "Nope. No shot. I'm not getting the plague."

"Actually, rats have surprisingly good hygiene—they groom themselves as much as cats do. There was one living in the wall in our basement when I was a kid." I smiled as the nearly forgotten memory took form. "I named him Walter. Get it? *Wall*-ter? Anyway—I woke up one night and saw him at the foot of my bed, just hanging out. Rats are chill."

Dan stared at me, mouth agape. "No. Shot," he restated firmly.

I chuckled, accepting the fact that I wouldn't win him over on this one.

Aside from the lone rodent, the rest of the house was unoccupied. As we made our way back downstairs, we pulled off whatever loose boards we could to open a few windows and allow for some airflow. Despite Dan's protest, it was a solid enough place to stay.

We reported back to the others, then started to get settled for the night. While Cap, Michelle, and Emma claimed the two bedrooms upstairs, the rest of us decided to get comfortable in the living room.

For a while, we just sat in silence, organizing our backpacks and setting up spare blankets on the floor to cushion the space. After a while, I noticed that Gabriela and Sander had crowded themselves into a corner of the room with their few belongings.

When we'd found out that it was The Community that had taken Alina, they had understandably been shaken. All night, and earlier that morning, Jason had been looking out for them. And with him gone, I'd felt a kind of responsibility to take over in his absence.

As I stood, there was movement in my peripheral. Sam. It looked like she'd had the same thought as I did—these kids could use someone right now.

"Are you two settling in okay?" Sam gave Sander and Gabriela a friendly smile as we approached. Golden-hour light filtered in through the window, highlighting the contours of her face, drenching her in the days' last rays of sunshine. I couldn't help staring at the way her rich, deep-umber skin shimmered, and the word "angelic" came to mind. It was more than fitting. Even through her own grief, Sam was still a beacon, spreading her light to those who needed it most.

"It's such a big space. Who needs so much of it?" Gabriela answered with wide brown eyes, her voice barely above a whisper as she picked at the loose medical tape holding the gauze in place on her neck. Emma had given Gabriela a painkiller before changing the dressing on her wound a little less than an hour ago, and judging by her wide pupils, the medicine had kicked in.

Sander raised his head at her words, confusion spreading across his face.

"Well, lucky for us, that means there's enough space to spread out and find the best spots to sleep." I crouched down so they didn't have to stretch their necks to look up. Sam followed, sitting cross-legged just a few feet away from Gabriela.

"I keep expecting another closet," the girl said, and I exchanged a surprised look with Sam as we both realized what she was referring to at the same time.

The space in this room, being around so many people—it was a stark contrast to her conditions at The Community. Sander had explained how his sister, Willa, had kept Gabriela locked up in the house Willa and Sander had shared—specifically, in Willa's bathroom closet.

A thought struck and I jumped to my feet.

"Hold on—I'll be right back." I quickly stepped over to the space I had claimed, grabbing the pillow I'd been planning on using that night, and carrying it back to Gabriela and Sander's corner. "Here, take this."

I placed the pillow next to Gabriela, creating a barrier between her and the rest of the room. "I'm sure it might take a bit of time to get used to the bigger space, but maybe that will help for tonight, at least."

Gabriela stared at the pillow for a moment, then wrapped her arms around it, wedging it closer to her body as she leaned against the wall. It was a big enough throw pillow that it covered most of her petite torso. As she hugged the pillow, her face softened, and she stared back at me with a small smile.

"Thank you," she murmured.

"Who's goin' to stay awake first tonight and make sure we weren't followed this time?" Sander interrupted.

I bristled at the question. I knew he hadn't meant it negatively— he'd expressed his apologies and appreciation in equal measure each time he had spoken with us. But I couldn't help feeling defensive, like it was a judgment on our group for what had happened. As much as I cared about keeping him safe, I still wasn't sure how much we could truly trust him. I couldn't help the quiet resentment that hovered just on the edge of my consciousness, knowing that the place he had come from, that his *sister*, was responsible for our group's loss.

"Bri and I are up first!" Sam proclaimed, and as Sander relaxed with the declaration, I felt guilty for getting annoyed in the first place. He was just looking for reassurance—same as the rest of us.

"Hey, Sander, if you want, you can hang out with us while we're on our shift. We can teach you how we've been looking out for the group. No pressure, but if you're interested?" Sam offered, and my eyes darted in her direction. If she noticed, she ignored my reaction.

Sander's eyes brightened as he sat up straighter, the corner of his mouth tugging into a small smile. "Y'all would really let me help? I mean, yeah! I-I'd really like to learn."

"That's the spirit!" Sam smiled back at him warmly. "We'll let you two finish settling in, for now!"

Sam stood, pulling me along with her. Once we were out of earshot, I leaned into her side. "That was a bold move back there."

She cocked an eyebrow. "Was it? He's scared. He doesn't trust us. And I can tell *some of us* don't really trust him, either."

"Was it that obvious?"

"Honestly, I'm surprised, Brian."

I sighed. "I know. I feel bad but . . . it's just hard to separate who he is from The Community."

"Even more reason to get to know him, and let him get to know us. Right?"

I couldn't argue against that logic. It wasn't long ago I had been saying something similar to Carter about Alina and Jason, after all. I tried to force myself to relax, remembering my own advice.

We were all strangers once. We take chances on people because that's *who we are.*

Considering where the last chance had left us, I still had doubts; but my trust in Sam was stronger.

"You're right, Sammy. If you think it's a good idea, I'll follow your lead."

"Of course it's a good idea." Sam threw a quick look over her shoulder before lowering her voice, leaning in. "Plus, you attract more bees with honey, right? Keep your potential enemies close and all that?" She raised an eyebrow before turning on her heel and casually walking away to find Russell.

I should have known Sam wouldn't just throw her trust into someone new. Her kindness was genuine, but she wasn't naive. She'd learned most of what she knew about survival from Carter, who believed in keeping more than a healthy bit of suspicion when it came to trusting someone new.

I thought back to when Sam and Carter had joined our group. We'd found Carter first, and within days, Sam had shown up. Carter was the first person she'd trusted. It had been weeks before she'd given anyone else more than one-word answers. Even longer before she'd given Dan, Russell, or me the time of day. But once we broke down her walls—or rather, once Russell finally annoyed her into submission—she'd quickly become the missing piece we hadn't known we were looking for. The four of us had been inseparable ever since.

I spied Dan setting up his space on the floor next to where I'd dropped my backpack. As I sat beside him, he bumped my foot with his. "What's going on over there?" He nodded toward Gabriela and Sander, who were talking quietly, seemingly more at ease.

"Sam and I were just checking in with them. Sander is going to join us for the first watch shift."

His lips tightened with concern, but he nodded.

He sat back, staring off like he always did when he was deep in thought. It was times like these where I wished I could see into his head. He kept so much of his thoughts just below the surface.

"You think they're okay?" he finally asked, and I knew he wasn't talking about the two teens across the room.

"I don't know." I was too tired to pretend to be optimistic. Now that we weren't moving, without the distraction that came with action, I couldn't keep the doubt at bay. "It depends on whether they actually stick to Cap's advice. But if I was in their shoes? If it was someone I loved like that?" I swallowed, unable to finish the statement. I wouldn't have hesitated to run off, either.

"*Love*? I mean, Jayce, yeah. But C? A bit early for love, don't you think?" Dan questioned.

"I don't know, man. When you know, you know, right?"

He paused, thinking for a moment before responding, "Okay, sure. It's obvious he feels something. But I doubt it's that deep. C was with her right before she was taken, right? He probably feels responsible and doesn't want J to get killed for it."

"Dark much?" I scoffed. "You've seen him when he's around her, though. Remember what he was like after the murder-pig attack? He was legit bleeding all over the place and wouldn't let go of Lee until Emma said she was okay. She had to *threaten* him to get him to let

Alina go so she could help him. And! He listened. When does Carter ever listen to *anything* Emma tells him to do?"

Dan laughed at my persistence. "Alright, Bri, I'll give you this one."

He rested on his elbows as he fell silent again, settling back into his thoughts. Though Dan didn't talk much about his feelings, I knew his tells. The way he'd stare off, seeming to forget the world around him. How his shoulders tensed, or the subtle ways his breathing changed. But I knew better than to push. He'd talk when he was ready.

I shifted to lie on my side, propping myself up on an elbow as I tried to get comfortable, waiting for him to open up the conversation again.

"If I'm being honest, I don't think Sam was wrong," Dan said. "I know this plan makes the most sense, but I hate the way it feels."

And as he said it out loud, I almost felt relieved that I wasn't the only one still thinking it. Almost. Because no matter what anyone said, it didn't change the reality of the situation.

I took a breath, opening the door for everything I had been keeping bottled up all day to finally be released. "I just keep thinking about how we lost three people today. Three of *us*. What if that was the last time—"

"You can't think like that. Once you go down that road..."

"I know. I just—" I couldn't finish the sentence. Because I knew that if it was Dan who'd been taken, I *wouldn't* be sitting here now. I would have gone after him, the same way Jason and Carter had run after Alina, even if no one followed.

No matter how hopeless, I wouldn't have hesitated.

"You know I'd do anything... I mean it," I managed to say before the rest of my words caught in my throat.

Dan's eyes met mine, and he reached over, gripping my hand. A serious expression fell across his face as he replied, "I know, B. And I'm here. I got you."

With his touch anchoring me back on solid ground, more than anything, I needed him to know. "Me too. I mean it. Always."

SEPTEMBER 2, 2025

WHEN I OPENED MY EYES, the sky was dusky on the cusp of sunrise. I reached behind my head, feeling around in the pocket of my backpack for my glasses case. As I slipped the glasses on, subtle movement at my side caught my attention.

"You're up early," Sam whispered from beside me. From the clarity in her voice, I assumed she'd been awake for a while, which wasn't like her.

I glanced at the empty sleep-space next to mine before remembering that Dan had the last night-watch shift with Russell—another reason why Sam was probably awake and, judging by the way her fingers tapped against her arm, restless. I shifted just enough so I could face her while still lying down.

"Did you even sleep?"

She shrugged half-heartedly, letting out a dramatic sigh. "A bit. You know how it is—first night in a new place. I can't stop thinking about Carter—not that I'm *not* thinking of Alina or Jason. I just can't believe he really left. On one hand, I admire him so much for going all-in. But on the other... I just selfishly wish he'd stayed."

I inhaled deeply, letting Sam's words settle before I quietly responded.

"I know. Me too. But..." I paused, thinking about how far Carter had come. Though Carter had a soft spot for Sam, opening up just enough to let her in, it was Alina who had truly begun to tear down his walls. "I'm also pretty damn proud of him."

"Yeah," she quietly agreed. "I knew he had it in him."

I smirked, unable to resist the urge to crack a joke. "What, a heart?"

When Carter and I had run into Jason and Alina in downtown Austin, he had all but demanded we leave the two of them there. It had been only a few days after the first hell-creature attack had left us with only eight survivors out of our twenty-two person group. The wounds had been—quite literally—still fresh. But once he'd started to spend time with her, things had changed. It was clear that Alina had opened up something inside him that no one else had been able to reach.

Sam laughed, caught off guard by my statement, and I grinned. We often resorted to joking through what we couldn't control. Which, if I was being honest, was quite a lot.

"Real talk, though?" I continued. "I'm kinda jealous. Like, where's my rugged apocalypse knight?"

Sam giggled. "I know! Like, Carter! Of all the people in our group." She paused, sighing. "It is kind of romantic, though. The two of them, going after her."

It was obvious Jason and Carter were at odds when it came to Alina, but they'd joined forces all the same. Jason always seemed to be two seconds away from dropping down on one knee when Alina was around. Watching the three of them had been like watching a rom-com unfold right before our eyes. Until The Community.

Until now.

The lightness I'd been feeling just a moment ago fell to the pit of my stomach.

"Bri..." Sam softly called, and her heartbreak echoed in my own chest.

She extended her hand, and I gently wrapped it in mine as she shifted closer, resting her head on my shoulder.

"I want to say it'll be okay, but it really doesn't feel that way," she said. "I can't stop thinking about what Alina must be going through—how scared she must be."

I squeezed her hand, wanting to say something reassuring, but unable to find the words. As we lay there, hands clasped, I couldn't help thinking that at least I wasn't waking up to worry alone. The moment was a much needed reminder that even in the hell we kept waking up to, we still had something good left—we still had each other.

After a few moments, Sam sat up. She removed her silk bonnet and shook out her curls, running a small bit of oil through her hair, the routine pure muscle memory.

Turning back to me, she asked, "How'd I do?"

I couldn't help smiling. "You are still the reigning champion of Best Apocalypse Hair Day."

Sam grinned, then grabbed my hand, pulling me upright to join her. "Let's go find Russell and Dan, then."

"You know Russell would still think you're the most gorgeous person on the planet no matter what you looked like, right?"

Sam swatted my shoulder. "Duh. As if Russell's opinion is what matters? This is for *me*. I just don't have a mirror, so I need *someone* to confirm for me."

She playfully stuck out her tongue as we headed toward the front of the house where we'd be most likely to find Russell and Dan.

Everyone had at least one "normal" routine that helped keep them anchored. The little things that someone else might find frivolous were quite often the one bright part in someone else's day. When we found Russell and Dan, they were each indulging in their own small pieces of normal.

"Xenomorph from *Alien*, a Yautja from *Predator*, or a hell-creature. You can't tell me a Yautja wouldn't win. Hell-creatures might have the height advantage, and Xenomorphs are fast, but Predator is a tank," Russell argued.

"Nah bro—Alien all the way. Chestbursters have the surprise attack. It isn't all about bulk," Dan retorted as he continued sketching in his notepad, leaning against the front door.

As soon as Russell saw Sam, he jumped up from his spot on the floor to meet her in the entryway. His face lit up, and in that moment it was like no one else existed as he wrapped his arms around her waist, pulling her in for a kiss.

Sam pushed away. "Ew, no! I still have morning breath!"

"I've smelled worse." Russell kissed her forehead and wrapped an arm around her shoulders as she jokingly swatted at his chest.

"So, we're still debating which extra-terrestrial would win in a fight?" I interrupted.

Dan raised an eyebrow, slipping his notepad back in his backpack and joining us in our circle. "Are you surprised?"

"Alright, boys—let's go outside. We don't want to wake up everyone else before sunrise." Sam ushered us out to sit on the edge of the front lawn by the walkway, where the grass wasn't as tall.

"So why are you two up so early?" Dan asked as he plucked a blade of grass, wrapping it around his finger.

"Oh, you know—depression spirals, catastrophizing, Brian snoring," Sam answered nonchalantly.

"The usual, then?" Dan's eyes crinkled as he held back a smile.

"Come on, I don't snore that bad," I protested, knowing I was one hundred percent lying. What could I say? No one's perfect. "At least I don't sleepwalk."

"Guys—it was *one* time! I swear, it was the mushrooms, dude," Russell burst out.

Sam leveled Russell with a look. "Everyone ate those mushrooms. They were *absolutely* the safe kind."

Russell pulled Sam into his lap, tickling her before she could say anything else in protest. She yelped, clasping a hand over her mouth to hold back a shriek of laughter as his fingers wriggled into her ribs.

"Ah! Not—not *fair!*" she squealed between fits of laughter.

"'Not not' is a double negative, which makes a positive—tickling is totally fair!" Russell crowed triumphantly.

"Told you he'd remember your lessons one day!" I called out to Sam, snickering.

All she could do was shriek in response.

Dan tilted his head closer to mine, lowering his voice as he wagered, "Five bucks this ends with Sam punching him."

"Five bucks? That's all you're willing to bet for an almost guaranteed win?"

Dan grinned, shrugging. "There's also a high chance she accidentally knees him in the balls trying to escape, so..."

No sooner had he said it, Russell yelped in pain, followed by Sam's profuse apologies.

"How does he *never* see it coming?" I wondered out loud.

Dan chuckled, and a burst of contentment warmed my chest. I leaned back to take in the first rays of sunrise coloring the horizon. Dan relaxed beside me and his expression softened as he stared at the soft pink and yellow lights of dawn illuminating the clouds. Whenever one of us was on the last night shift, we always made it a point to watch the sunrise together. All too often, it was the only moment of tranquility we had for the day.

Dan's shoulder bumped into mine, and the corner of my mouth tilted into a smile as I leaned against him. I was so ready to settle in and soak up every last second before the day officially began.

All of a sudden, Russell practically dove on top of me, slamming me against Dan.

"Help," he whined, pressing his forehead to my shoulder. "I think she broke me."

"Oh, buddy. Maybe next time try a different tactic?" I patted the top of his head sympathetically, barely holding back another laugh.

Sam wrapped her arms around Russell from behind, cringing guiltily. "Just... try to focus on the sunrise."

"Why, so you can finish me off in peace?" Russell sputtered, clinging to my shirt.

Dan pulled his arm from where it was trapped between us, laying it across my shoulders as we tried not to laugh at Russell's misfortune.

"I swear you four are like a pile of golden retriever puppies," Emma's voice called from the front door. Though a statement like that from her would usually carry an air of sarcasm, this time her words were laced with affection.

Emma sauntered over to our group, plopping down right in front of us as she tilted her freckled face to the hint of sun in the sky. Her silky auburn hair seemed to ignite with the morning light. I studied her for a moment, trying to gauge her mood, but she looked... calm.

It was a far cry from the devastated silence she'd carried all day yesterday.

Russell sat up, dramatically blinking and rubbing his eyes. With a gasp, he exclaimed, "Red? With us? Of her own free will? Man, you really must have been hit hard."

"*Russell!*" Sam gasped as Dan exclaimed, "*Really*, bruh?"

But, to our surprise, Emma burst out laughing. I stared, unsure what to do with the uncharacteristic response.

"See? Red's vibing. It's all good, fam. Chill!" Russell replied with a lopsided grin.

"Oh, it's definitely far from all good," Emma responded with a scoff. "But I came here for a distraction. So—distract. Entertain me. Be your weird selves."

Dan tensed at my side, and I shifted awkwardly, exchanging an uncomfortable look with Sam, as I tried to figure out how to react. Thankfully, Russell didn't miss a beat.

"Oh! I know just the thing. Okay, Red. Who would win in a fight: Alien, Predator, or a hell-creature?"

"Predator, duh." Emma rolled her eyes.

"That's what I said! Hell fucking yeah, Red! That's what I'm talking about!" Russell raised both fists in the air.

"Red and Russ on the same side? I never thought I'd see the day." Dan shook his head in mock-disbelief.

"We're only on the same side because I didn't know who he'd already chosen," Emma groaned.

Russell moved to Emma's side, wrapping an arm around her shoulders. She responded to the gesture with a semi-horrified expression. Bickering had been Emma and Russell's primary form of communication since the day they'd met, and I was honestly shocked she'd let him get as close as he was now.

But of course, Russell didn't stop there.

"Do you feel that, Red?" he asked slyly, squeezing her in a half hug.

"I know I'm going to regret asking, but—feel *what*?"

"A life-long friendship? The next dynamic duo? Best bros in the making? Take your pick. Admit it—deep down, you knew this day would come." Russell gave her a crooked smile.

Emma grimaced, but the hint of a smile pulled at the corner of her mouth. Clearly, Russell saw it too, taking it as a sign of encouragement as he continued, "Honestly, you're better off not fighting it."

Dan's chest pressed against the back of my shoulder as he leaned forward to catch Emma's line of sight, teasing, "Yeah, Red. You're stuck with him forever now."

"Okay, okay. Fine. As long as he doesn't start asking to braid my hair," Emma finally relented.

When we finally headed back inside, Cap and Michelle were already at work poring over a map. Russell and Sam jumped into their assigned task of re-calculating our inventory and rations for our new headcount, while Emma dragged Dan over to wake up Gabriela and Sander, insisting she needed to teach Dan how to check stitches. Apparently Gabriela was to be her guinea pig. All things considered, it was probably a good idea—we'd been relying on Emma for most of our medical needs, and if yesterday's events had taught us anything, it was that we needed to be prepared for any sudden changes.

I decided to busy myself cleaning up the sleep space in the living room, arranging the backpacks by the front door next to the spot where Cap and Michelle had placed theirs. I'd expected the small chore to prompt something like muscle memory, reminding me of what our days used to be like when we were constantly on the move. Instead, as I noticed everyone else involved in their own tasks within their small groups, I couldn't help feeling like I had no idea what I was supposed to be doing.

I felt... lost.

I tried not to let my insecurity creep back in. It didn't happen often, but the twisting of uncertainty in my stomach was more than reminiscent of times past where I had been left scrambling as everyone else had moved forward.

"There has to be a way we can find people like us. People who want to help." Michelle's exasperated voice carried from down the hall.

Pushing the insecurity back into hiding, I followed the echoes of conversation to where Cap and Michelle had been working.

"What's going on?" I asked, stepping into the room.

"Well, if I'm being honest, not much," Michelle huffed.

"We're trying to figure out where we'll be most likely to find allies," Cap explained, pinching the bridge of their nose in concentration. "But it's not like we can pinpoint a spot on a map to find the people we need. It's about where they'd have gone, not where they were before."

"Is that a riddle?" Russell asked as he and Sam strolled into the room with Emma, Sander, Dan, and Gabriela close on their heels.

"If only it were that easy," Cap lamented. "I'm talking about the people I used to know from the bushcraft groups I was a part of."

"I swear I've never missed social-fucking-media more than I do now," Emma mumbled.

"Why social media?" Michelle frowned.

"Well, for one, we could stalk people's profiles and learn about them without having to talk to them. It's honestly amazing how much you could figure out about a person just from digging into their post history. We'd also be able to just shoot out a message into the void and hashtag join-the-resistance or whatever. It'd be way easier to filter out sketchy motherfuckers, too. The last thing we need is another Willa." Emma cringed, shooting a look at Sander. "No offence."

Sander winced at the mention of his sister, his gaze drifting to the ground. Gabriela gave his shoulder a sympathetic squeeze.

"We need some way to get through to the groups who are most likely to help. Like, a people filter," Cap thought out loud.

"I was always a fan of the filters that make your eyes and mouth really big. Or like, the one that gave you demon horns," Russell said.

"Dude." Dan leveled him with a look.

Russell rolled his eyes. "*Dude*. I know they're not talking about *that* kind of filter. I was just saying—"

"LoRa!" Cap exclaimed, their eyes lit up with excitement.

"Laura?" Sam's brow furrowed.

"Oh! Oh!" Michelle exclaimed. "The off-grid, mesh-texty-radio thing!"

"Exactly! It would be perfect—I mean, if they're still using it. And if we can get through—this could be our answer!"

"Okay—what in the world are you two talking about? Because what *I'm* hearing is that Cap has a friend named Laura who runs an off-grid text-chain club," Emma interrupted, holding her head in both hands.

"Yeah, uh, can you maybe E-L-I-5 this for us?" I jumped in.

"E-L-I-5? Ell-eh-five? Ellis? I'm sorry, now I'm lost," Michelle answered.

"It means 'explain like I'm five,'" Dan translated.

"Okay, let's start over." Cap clapped their hands, grabbing our attention back. "So, what we need is to be able to target our communications and reach the right people—right? And we need something that doesn't require Wi-Fi or electricity or cell service. Something *off-grid*. Before the invasion, I was researching how to get started with my own LoRa—that means long-range—meshtastic device for, well, situations like this."

"So, this is something that already exists? Like, other people might be using it? How does it work?" Sam asked.

"Yes! How do I explain this?" Cap's brow wrinkled as they took a second. "Okay, so you know how walkie-talkies work? Now imagine that those walkie-talkies could connect to *any other* walkie-talkie in range and pass on your message. But, instead of transmitting your voice, it sends a text message. Then the recipient's device acts as a jump-off point to pass on the text to the next device in range. Now, it's a long-shot. But a buddy from one of my groups told me all about how *his* group planned on using them in emergency situations."

Cap grinned from ear to ear, and even though I still wasn't one hundred percent sure how or *if* it would work, their enthusiasm was contagious. My heart raced at the realization that we could have the answer to all of our problems after one night. Or, well, at least *some* of our problems. The more I thought about it, the more I decided it was the best lead we could have hoped for.

"Okay, so let me get this straight," Emma jumped in. "We're going to shoot a message into the airwaves and hope that Cap's little off-grid anti-government survivalist buddies pick up the phone?"

"Hell yeah! We're totally going to raise a rebel army of anarchists!" Russell cheered.

"Isn't 'rebel' and 'anarchist' kind of the same thing?" Dan asked.

"Not technically—" Sam started to answer as Cap interjected, "That's not exactly what I meant—"

"Say no more—I'm all in," Russell eagerly interrupted. "I always wanted to get down with anarchists. Who else? Let's vote!"

Sam and Michelle raised their hands first. I looked at Dan, gauging his reaction. He met my gaze, shrugging as a half smile tugged at the corner of his mouth. His eyes were bright, lit up with newfound hope. We both raised our hands at the same time, and Sander and Gabriela were close behind on the vote.

The only one left was Emma.

"Cap, I love you. You know I respect you and think you're, like, the smartest person to walk this planet. But we don't even know if these people are still alive. We're really going to put all of our eggs in a basket that's basically being held together with hopes and dreams? What happens if it doesn't work? We aren't exactly operating on an endless amount of fucking time. We don't even *have* this device, or know where to find one. You're going to risk my brother's life on a hunch? And Alina's? *Carter's*?!" The fire in her eyes had returned— wild, consuming, verging on dangerous.

Michelle started, "Emma, I know you're—"

"No, Chelle." Emma pointed a finger in Michelle's direction. "Don't write this off as me being caught up in my *feelings*. The longer we wait, the less likely we are to see them again. Hell knows the kind of torture Alina is going through. Jason will only become their next science experiment if they're caught, and I can't even imagine what they'll do to Carter! You know, I didn't expect anyone else to *really* give a shit about Jason or Alina. I get it. You just met them. They're more disposable to you. It's why you all so easily came to the conclusion that we had to move on without Alina in the fucking *first* place. But I *never* thought you'd risk Carter's life like this."

"Emma, that's not how we feel at all," Cap tried to counter.

"I'm not done talking! And it might not be how you *feel*, but it's still the plan you all decided on long before Jason and Carter said they were going off to find her." She jabbed a finger at us, narrowing her eyes. "It's the plan *all of you* are still trying to fucking rationalize! If we were going to decide on a plan based off of bullshit and vibes, we could have just gone with Jason and Carter in the fucking first place!"

The group was frozen, stunned by Emma's outburst. Her words cut deep, tearing our small buds of blooming hope into ribbons.

Emma exhaled roughly, her voice thick with emotion as she added, "Well, you might as well leave me here, too. Hell knows, I should never have left *them* in the first place. I'll figure out a way back and find them. I'm done." She stormed toward the backyard, leaving us standing there, speechless.

After a moment, Michelle broke our stunned silence as she stammered, "I should go after her. I should—"

"It's okay, Chelle," Dan delicately interrupted. It was clear Michelle was hurt by the outburst. Emma had never yelled at her or Cap like that before. "You stay here. I got her." Before anyone could object, he jogged after Emma.

I'd thought that maybe, with how the day had started, we were ready to move forward—that with a new plan we would be able to reignite the fire that kept us going. But nothing was ever that simple.

The wounds were still open and raw, too deep to have healed so quickly. And it would be a long time before we would be able to take a step forward without looking over our shoulders for what had been left behind.

I sank back into the pit that guilt had started digging the morning before, deep enough now to swallow me whole.

As I went through the motions of talking through our new plan with everyone else, my mind stayed with Dan and Emma.

Emma was always the first to admit she was "feral on a good day," with an intensity that was always dialed up to one hundred. It translated into how she treated her patients in our camp, too—she was scarily protective over them. Think: Grizzly bear in the form of a petite, 5'2", red-haired woman—except her cubs were our sick and injured camp members.

After Dan's leg had been wounded by the hell-creature that had attacked our camp, he had been no exception to the rule. And through the forced proximity, he'd genuinely become friends with Emma. Dan had a knack for bringing the calm, which was exactly what Emma needed now—especially since her two most important people weren't here. He'd find a way to talk her down and get her back on board.

Still, I couldn't help the unease that twisted tighter in my stomach the longer it took for them to return.

When Emma and Dan finally rejoined the group, Emma made a beeline for Gabriela and Sander, insisting that she needed to check Gabriela's stitches—even though she'd already given Gabriela a checkup not even an hour prior. Though none of us questioned her outright, I caught Michelle and Cap watching Emma with the same concerned look I was trying to keep from my face.

But the activity was keeping her calm and Gabriela seemed to appreciate the extra attention, asking Emma questions the whole time. And as Emma answered her with the blunt honesty she was infamous for, Sander started to relax. I guessed he hadn't received much transparency back at The Community, so for him, Emma's tendency to overstate her intentions was likely a welcome change.

So, as much as it seemed like overkill, everyone just looked the other way.

Was it the best way to deal with the situation? Probably not. But we were stuck in an impossible balancing act trying to give Emma the leeway she needed to process, while also keeping the peace, and making sure our next steps were the right ones.

At last, Cap beckoned everyone over to the cars, indicating it was time to head out.

Emma got into the back of the SUV with Sander and Gabriela, and Dan slid into the driver's seat. As Russell and Sam climbed into the truck with Cap, I caught Michelle warily eyeing the other car.

I tried to be casual as I met Michelle in the middle of the two vehicles, just in case Emma was watching. "Don't worry, Chelle. Dan and I will look out for her. She'll be okay."

Michelle was quiet for an extended breath before she finally met my eyes, "Emma is... she's going through a lot. She needs all of the support she can get. I just hope we have enough to give."

"Well, luckily I have more than enough to go around," I responded with forced positivity, hoping our resident psychologist wouldn't see straight through me.

Michelle didn't call me out directly, but it was clear she didn't buy my confidence for a second as she wrapped me in a tight hug. "I don't doubt you do, you wonderful human. Just don't forget to take care of your heart as well."

She squeezed me one last time before stepping away.

Ready or not, we were moving on to the next part of our journey.

SEPTEMBER 4, 2025

"How is that an elephant?" Russell argued.

"Ears. Trunk. Hooves." Sander punctuated each word with the tap of his pen against the notebook Russell had stolen from Sam. They'd been playing car games for the better part of the day, and their arguments had only gotten more ridiculous the longer we were on the road.

"Elephants don't have hooves. They have toes," Gabriela chimed in. "But other than that, it looks like a pretty decent elephant to me."

I glanced at Sam, who was sitting in the passenger seat while I drove. Her lips pressed together in a firm line with her jaw clenched tight as she watched the trio in the back seat through the rearview mirror.

"Whatever. Pass it over. It's my turn again," Russell dismissed the other two.

Sam's eyes widened as she whipped around, twisting in her seat to snatch the notebook from Sander's hand before Russell could grab it. "Oh no, you don't."

"Babe, come on! Just one more game!" Russell whined.

"You've already had five 'last games,' *babe*. Find something else to do. Preferably, something that doesn't waste any more pages in my *journal*."

"Maybe we can use the notebooks from Dr. Creepazoid," Russell suggested. "What happened to those, anyway?"

"They are safely tucked away in the truck, and there is no way Michelle will let you anywhere near them," I answered. "She's trying to figure out what makes this self-proclaimed 'doctor' tick... or at least understand why he's still experimenting on people without the invaders forcing him to."

"He *is* a real doctor, you know. He used to be a professor and do research at the university. Willa would talk about how smart he was all the time," Sander spoke up from the back seat. He'd been joining in on our conversations more, asserting his knowledge when he knew he could contribute.

Sander hadn't just stolen the notebooks from The Community's alien-worshipping cult leader—he'd read each one front to back, and had them practically memorized. Originally I'd tried to take on interpreting the stolen notebooks' contents with his help, but I'd quickly realized that the material was above my paygrade. It was less "scientific journal" and more "sociopathic manifesto from a man with the biggest God-complex I'd ever come across," which made it way more Michelle's wheelhouse than mine.

I smiled to myself as I remembered what Michelle had said as she had taken over the task. *At least a PHD in psychology is still worth something after the apocalypse.*

"So how did he go from being a professor to Dr. Frankenstein?" Sam asked.

"I thought Frankenstein was the monster?" Russell interrupted.

"Frankenstein was the doctor. His monster doesn't actually have a name," Sander answered.

"That's right! Glad to see *someone* else in this car has read the classics!" Sam's voice immediately perked up as she turned in her seat to grin at Sander.

I looked in the rearview mirror just in time to see a flush of pink spread across Sander's cheeks, highlighted by a sheepish smile from the praise. Over the last few days, we'd been breaking through the hard shell he hid under, smoothing out his scowl lines and finding the kid underneath.

"Damn, Sandman. Are you trying to steal my girl with that book-talk?" Russell joked, ruffling Sander's hair before the teen had time to panic at the fake accusation.

"I never read the book," Gabriela mused. "I watched the movie with my dads, though. Well, it was *Young Frankenstein*, but that counts, right?"

"*Put... zee candle... BACK!*" I quoted in a fake German accent, cackling to myself.

"Yeah! That's the one!" Gabriela cheered from the back seat.

Soon enough, the conversation faded into a mosaic of favorite quotes from other movies and TV shows, and it was honestly the perfect kind of background noise for driving.

After a while I realized that Sam had grown quiet, and wasn't participating in the conversation. I glanced over to find her staring blankly at her open notebook.

"So, how's *Sam's History Of the World* coming along?" I asked.

Sam blinked as my question shook her from wherever her train of thought had been heading. She sighed, closing the notebook. "Well, actually, I'm trying something new. It's a letter. To Carter. Michelle thinks it'll help."

While we were all committed to moving forward, trying to track down the folks Cap knew from their network, the absence of our friends was never far from our minds.

Emma was either a hurricane of emotion, or silently going through the motions. Having Gabriela to care for and Michelle to keep her talking helped, but lately it seemed that Dan was the only person she actually *wanted* to spend time with.

Sam, though—her sadness hung like a shadow, always there, and weighing heavier each day. I hadn't realized just how close she and Carter had been until after he'd left. I couldn't fill the space he usually occupied, but at least I could be there for her.

"So, is it helping?" I asked

"I don't know, honestly. It feels weird writing a letter I'll never mail, but it's not that different from how I've already been using my journal." Sam shrugged, hugging the notebook to her chest. "Ask me again in a few days."

"Fair enough." I tapped the steering wheel with my fingers, returning my focus to the road. We hadn't been driving nearly as long a stretch this time, but already I was itching for the next break.

Yesterday, we'd been able to check out a homesteading space where some of Cap's acquaintances would sometimes spend their time. And, while we had found people there, they hadn't been the people we'd been looking for. They had been kind enough, if a bit untrusting—but, then again, so had we.

I'd expected to feel more nervous the first time we ran into another group, but the encounter hadn't come with the same bone-chilling nerves The Community had inspired. We had only stayed long enough to exchange information, though we hadn't learned anything new. The only positive that had come out of the conversation was that we had been able to warn a few more people about The Community. Whether they had believed us or not was another story.

In the end, we'd helped them jump a car, bartering for food from their garden in return. Then, we'd said goodbye. It had been a bit anti-climactic, but I didn't mind the lack of excitement. It reminded me of when we'd cross random groups of people in the earlier days of the invasion—back when fear wasn't the first emotion that came with meeting others.

Dan's voice over the walkie-talkie interrupted my trailing thoughts.

"Car two—come in. Over."

"We're here, what's up? Over," Sam answered.

"Fuel and supply run in the next fifteen. Over."

"Got it. Over and out."

"That was quick," Gabriela noted.

I glanced at the fuel gauge on the SUV and noted that we were just dipping below the ¾ mark. "Well, the next location we're headed toward is kind of in the middle of nowhere. Cap is probably just trying to play it super safe with our fuel supply."

When we did finally pull off the road, hitting one of the smaller towns along our route, I could only stare at our destination, deeply confused. This was not what I'd been expecting.

Cap, however, was almost giddy as we piled out of our cars to gather in front of a sketchy-looking building with a giant sign that read **Discount Electronics** in a blocky comic sans style font. The windows were peppered with homemade sale signs, complete with graphics that looked like they had been hand-drawn in MS Paint. It was certainly... a choice. The parking lot was empty, but the building seemed to be in good-enough shape. At least from the outside.

"Uh, Cap?" I tried to find a way to phrase my question with tact, but before I could find the words, Emma interjected.

"Why are we at a store that looks like the reincarnation of my fifth-grade science project PowerPoint?"

"It's a used electronics store! The one I was *just* talking about in the car," Cap exclaimed, gesturing to the building. "You know, for the radio!"

"So is this, like, an undercover hideout for the anarchists to trade top-secret off-grid technology?" Russell skeptically eyed the building.

"No, no. Nothing so exciting." Cap chuckled. "It's just a used electronics store. But I remember someone specifically mentioning that this place collected pieces that could be used for the LoRa meshtastic device I was telling you about."

"*If* this is the right place," Michelle added.

"I'm telling you, this is it!"

From the way Dan sighed and Emma rolled her eyes, I had a feeling this wasn't the first time Michelle had emphasized that particular disclaimer. It wouldn't be the first time we'd gotten a location wrong, either, as Cap had needed to rely on their memory when making their list of stops.

"Okay, so what's the plan? What are we looking for?" Sam steered the conversation back on track.

"And does the plan include lunch? I'm starving," Russell added, clutching his stomach dramatically.

"I think we can divide and conquer," Cap thought out loud. "Sam, Michelle, and... Sander. Why don't y'all come with me, and the rest of you can get lunch together."

Sander's eyes widened, but he eagerly shot to attention, joining the others as they headed toward the store.

"Wait! Don't forget your lockpick MVP! I'm coming, too!" Russell jogged after them.

"What happened to being *staaaarving*?" Emma muttered under her breath.

"Did you want your new BFF to be your sous chef too, Red?" Dan smirked, bumping her shoulder.

I expected a sarcastic remark in return, but instead Emma's face relaxed as she snorted a laugh. "Yeah, it's probably better if he goes and plays MacGyver with Cap."

"What's MacGyver?" Gabriela asked, her eyes flitting between Dan and Emma.

Emma froze before releasing a dramatic sigh. "Thank you for the reminder that I am old as fuck. Come with me, babe. Help me grab the food and I'll teach you about the olden times."

Gabriela smiled, trailing behind Emma back to the truck.

I watched them retreat, relieved to see Emma was in a decent mood. While Emma and Gabriela dug through our supplies, I turned my attention to Dan.

His eyes were trained on the truck, watching as Emma emphatically explained something to the girl. The corner of his mouth tipped up, amusement briefly crossing his face.

I took a step closer, lowering my voice before commenting, "She seems better today, yeah?"

Dan nodded, watching them a moment longer before finally pulling his gaze away.

"Yeah. For now, at least. She's usually alright during the day, but you know how it goes."

"Well, hey, why don't you take a break and switch with Gabriela or something when we get in the cars again?" I suggested, completely not for selfish reasons. Since being back on the road, Dan had opted for traveling with Emma, Michelle, and Cap. That had left me as the point person for the other car. As much as I loved everyone in our group, I wasn't used to spending so much time apart from Dan.

"Nah, it's fine. It's probably better if I stay close enough to help her when she needs it." Dan shifted his weight from one foot to the other. His eyes darted in the direction of the truck, just briefly, before he forced a nonchalant shrug. "Nothing to worry about. It's all good, B."

As much as he insisted things were alright, his body language screamed otherwise. But before I could say anything to try and convince him differently, Emma called us over to help divide the food she and Gabriela had put together.

The afternoon sun was starting to feel uncomfortably hot as it beat down on my shoulders, and my T-shirt chafed at the back of my neck, suddenly feeling too tight. The abrupt way Dan had brushed off my invitation shouldn't have bothered me as much as it did. He was looking out for a friend. That was all. And clearly, judging by Emma's body language, the gentle way she joked around with Gabriela, and overall demeanor, the support seemed to be helping.

I hung back at the edge of the tailgate, trying to force my thoughts elsewhere. My eyes drifted to the store, studying the windows for the shadows of our friends moving inside. They hadn't been gone long, but each time we separated, my nerves went into overdrive. I couldn't see inside the store from where we were standing, and as much as I tried to focus my hearing, they were moving so quietly that the place might as well have been empty.

"What do you think is taking them so long?" Gabriela's soft voice pulled my attention back.

"Aside from the fact that the store should have probably closed down before the world ended?" Emma snarked, hopping down from the tailgate. "Honestly, considering we sent all of our tech geeks inside a gadgets and gizmos store, they're probably having the time of their lives digging through whatever is in there. They haven't been gone that long. I wouldn't worry."

"Where do you think we're going to go after this?" Gabriela asked.

"Well, Cap wants to build up our fuel supply," Dan answered. "Some more food wouldn't hurt, either. Not sure what other supplies we're low on, but Cap was saying anytime we stop we should try and re-up."

"Is it me, or are they being more cautious than usual?" I asked.

Cap was always one to plan ahead, but the fact that we were placing so much emphasis on building up supplies and being so conservative with gas had me questioning just how long they expected our mission to take.

"I mean, are you really surprised?" Emma raised an eyebrow. "Listen, I'm no Michelle, but I recognize trauma coping when I see it. Controlling what they can control or whatever. Probably overcompensating for the fact that this mission is fucked and going nowhere."

A twinge of frustration prickled in my chest as I took a breath, focusing on keeping a measured tone as I responded, "Well, I wouldn't say going nowhere. They got us this far, didn't they?"

"Bravo, then. A shop full of junk," Emma scoffed. "Until we actually find something that will help Jason, Alina, and Carter, consider me unimpressed."

"Come on, Emma. That isn't fair. We're just getting started."

"Not fair? You want to know what isn't fair? Jason and Carter alone in Central Texas on a half-baked rescue mission while our group plays around in a deserted electronics store."

Gabriela's shoulders tensed as her eyes darted between us. I opened my mouth to respond, but Dan jumped in first, changing the subject before I could argue back.

"B, help me put some of this extra stuff in the SUV's trunk."

My stomach sank as I caught his eye and noticed the way his jaw tensed. He was... mad? Frustrated?

Reluctantly, I nodded, taking the duffle bag he held out to me, and started walking to the SUV.

He rounded to the other side of the car, and I followed, all the while replaying my words to figure out what I'd said that was so wrong. I thought I'd been diplomatic—advocating for Cap, who'd always done right for us in the past. If anything, I'd held back. My mind drifted to what I'd *wanted* to say—

We're doing all of this for you! For Carter. For Alina. For Jason.

Tell us you have a better plan to rescue them.

If you just took one second to think about someone else, maybe—

The last thought stopped me in my tracks, guilt punching through my stomach. Or maybe it was the look on Dan's face.

"Go easy on her, B. She doesn't mean it."

He was taking her side?

I let out a sharp exhale, failing to mask my frustration. "It's not fair for her to talk about Cap like that. They don't deserve it. They're trying. We all are."

"I know that. And I'm not saying you're wrong. I'm just saying, she's struggling. I'm asking you to try and understand." The calm tone in his voice contrasted the rigidness in his posture, and all of my counterarguments turned to sand on my tongue.

Was I wrong to argue with her? What she'd said had been uncalled for and critical. From the look on Gabriela's face, Emma hadn't been doing a great job helping us instill confidence in our plans for our newer and more impressionable camp members, either. Was Cap's plan perfect? No. But it was the best lead we had. It wasn't as if anyone else had better ideas. And we had to start somewhere. Not every problem could be solved overnight.

Taking a breath, I finally responded, "So we're just supposed to let her talk shit? Not call her out on it? Let her do or say whatever she wants because she's upset?"

"No, I'm not saying that." Dan rubbed the back of his neck, taking a moment to find his words. "I'm just saying, now isn't the time to argue with her. She can't hear what you're saying when she gets all worked up. Just... give her space."

I considered his words, taking in the tightness of his jaw, the worry lines across his brow. Dan hated conflict. The fact that he'd even taken me aside to try to advocate for Emma spoke volumes. If it were anyone else but Dan, I might have pushed back harder. But I trusted his judgment. I trusted him.

"Alright. Okay. If you say so."

At my response, some of the tension left his body.

"I'll talk to her, okay?" he compromised.

I nodded, but on the inside, I couldn't keep my doubts at bay.

We were only at the beginning of this mission. If we kept fighting amongst ourselves, if we started questioning each other, it would only hold us all back. I knew that was part of why Dan had said what he had. Still. It didn't sit right.

I couldn't help feeling that our group was fracturing right before my eyes. We were in pieces, stretching to conceal the spaces left behind, and only time would tell whether the bonds would settle or snap.

SEPTEMBER 6, 2025

"STAY BACK!" the stranger growled, aiming a gun our way. "We don't have anything worth taking." His arms shook, lips quivering around the threat. Behind him, two small faces peered out of an abandoned car's window.

They couldn't have been more than seven—a little girl and a little boy. Their dark hair was sweat-soaked, framing their faces as hot tears carved trails through the dirt on their faces, revealing dark honey-colored skin underneath. But as scared as they looked, they didn't dare open their mouths to make a sound. My stomach churned as I tried to pull my eyes away from the two children shut inside the hot vehicle.

When had we stopped to see if they needed help? How long had it been since he had shoved them in the car, slamming the door shut? Had we made a mistake? How much time did they have before the heat got to them?

"We just stopped to help, I swear." Russell held out his hands, still trying to offer a bottle of water. "Just take the water. Please?"

I tensed beside him, and he subtly shifted in front of me, keeping his focus on the man standing in front of the car.

I knew Sam, Emma, and Dan had their eyes fixed on us from inside our SUV, but I didn't dare turn around to check on them. Every once in a while, their voices would carry as they argued behind the closed doors.

Maybe stopping had been a bad idea. Maybe I should have kept going. But I couldn't just drive past—not when it looked like this guy was seconds away from keeling over. How could I ignore the kids with their dirt-streaked faces and torn clothes, desperately trying to help drag bags down the deserted road?

"Please, sir—you gotta open that door," I begged.

He froze for a moment, and his Adam's apple bobbed in his throat as he swallowed hard. Finally, he lowered the gun, wiping the back of his hand across his sunburned forehead. Choking on a breath, he took a few steps backward, fumbling behind him for the door handle. The two kids scrambled out from the back seat and clung to the man's legs with their tiny arms, breathing heavily from the heat.

"That's it, man. See? We aren't moving," Russell reassured him.

My breath shook as I said, "Russell is going to roll the bottle of water over."

The man eyed the bottle, unable to hold back the reflexive way his tongue swept over his dry lips as he swallowed thickly. He nodded, tossing the gun to the side, sinking to the ground. Russell didn't hesitate before rolling the bottle, and I grabbed his arm, towing him back toward our truck to create some more distance.

"Wait," Russell called, pulling away from me before I could stop him. "We might be able to get that car to work. If you let us."

The man eyed us as the kids passed the bottle back and forth, taking small sips.

Finally, after a long pause, he asked, "Why?"

"Because you need help," Russell answered, shrugging.

The man's initial panic had melted into a pool of exhaustion. He limply gestured to the weapon.

"The last people who stopped were... If I hadn't had that gun, I don't know what they'd have done. You know, that thing isn't even loaded?" His shoulders heaved as he took a deep, shuddering breath. "I thought—I thought you'd be like them."

"Well, fuck them. We're good guys," Russell blurted before shooting a look at the children, cringing. "Sorry for the f-bomb."

"We'll get you and your kids set up and ready to go, no strings," I reassured the stranger.

"The kids. They're not even mine," the man whispered. "Somehow, I'm all they have and they aren't even mine."

As hard as we pushed for them to join us, the stranger refused. He didn't even share his name. In the end, we left them with all of the food and water we could spare, an extra container of gas, and a working car. It was all we could do.

It wasn't the first time we'd come across someone who was reluctant to accept help. And I knew I shouldn't take it personally. Their distrust said more about their experiences than it did about us. Still. I wanted to do more, and I hated that we had to leave them like that.

Emma was the first to break the silence from the passenger seat up front next to Dan, who had taken over driving.

"We should have just taken the kids."

"I'm pretty sure kidnapping is still frowned upon," Sam muttered with a sigh. She'd just stopped staring out the window behind us and settled against Russell's shoulder. At the mention of the kids, she twisted in her seat to peer out the window once more, as if hoping the man might have changed his mind and started following our car.

"And child endangerment isn't?" Emma scoffed. "I mean, really. If we hadn't stopped, that guy was days, possibly *hours*, from dying and leaving those children stranded."

"And now they're not," Russell bluntly cut in. "Thanks to us. Now he can take care of those kids better than he could before."

"Until the next time he threatens someone with an unloaded gun and they call his bluff. We should have taken those kids."

Russell opened his mouth, but Sam stopped him from saying whatever was going to come next with a gentle hand on his arm. Russell huffed, loudly settling back in the seat, but he didn't push further.

The truth was, we didn't live in a world of rights and wrongs anymore. We could only hope that when we made a choice, it didn't lead to something worse. It didn't make the decisions any easier, though.

"We should check in with the other car," Dan changed the subject. "Red, you want to grab the walkie from the glove box?"

Emma dug through the compartment, pushing around the few emergency supplies we had inside so she could free the walkie-talkie. We hadn't been that far behind the others, and it was a bit odd that we hadn't heard from them yet.

The last time we'd checked in, we'd told them that we were going to pull off to help the man and his kids, and that we'd catch up. We hadn't anticipated that it'd be such an extended stop, though.

"Car one, come in. Over," Emma called.

Static buzzed from the other side, blending with the sounds of our car rumbling down the deserted road.

"Cap. Michelle. Come in. Over," Emma tried again, only to be answered with more white noise.

"Maybe we're too far?" Sam suggested, not even trying to hide the worry that shook her tone.

"Or maybe we're just fucked. Everything is always fucked," Emma muttered.

"Red, come on—can you chill for like, ten seconds?" Russell burst out. "We get it—you've given up or whatever. But the rest of us are still here trying."

"Back off, Russ." Dan glared through the rearview mirror at Russell, a warning flickering in his eyes.

"*I'm* not the one constantly telling everyone else that we're 'fucked,' or that we're making all the wrong choices, or attacking everyone else for just fucking trying."

Emma whipped around in her seat as she hurled her words like weapons. "No. *You* are the one stuck in a fantasy world thinking that everything will be just fine if we all hold hands and *vibe*. *Fuck off*, Russell."

"No. You don't get to talk to me like that," Russell replied, deadly serious.

My heart jumped as the car jerked to a sudden stop, the seatbelt tightening against my chest, locking me in place. Next to me, Sam gasped as Russell threw his arm across her to help brace against the sudden change in momentum.

"What the *fuck*, Dan?" Russell growled.

"I said *back off*," Dan responded through gritted teeth, leveling Russell with a look that I had never seen on his face before.

For a moment, all I could do was blink in shock. I knew I should say something to try and deescalate the situation, but as I stared at Dan, seeing all warmth stripped from his expression, my words lodged in my throat like cement.

Luckily, Sam had enough of her wits about her to step in.

"Everyone—just *stop!*" With all eyes on her, she continued in a softer tone, "This isn't easy for any of us. But, you guys—we're on the same team. It's hard, and it's not going to get any easier, but if we're taking out all of our anger on each other and jumping down each other's throats, we might as well stay right here on the side of the road and wait for the next threat to come finish us all off."

Russell and Dan continued glaring at each other in tense silence until Emma reached over to squeeze Dan's hand, drawing his attention away. He studied Emma for a moment, before something in their quiet exchange allowed for him to release the rest of the emotion that had hardened him.

"I'm sorry," Emma said as she let go of Dan's hand, turning around to look at Sam and Russell. "I know I've been really hard to be around. It might not look like it, but I'm trying."

Russell's shoulders relaxed, but his voice still held an edge as he stiffly responded, "I'm sorry, too."

Before anyone could say anything else, the walkie-talkie crackled to life.

"Car two. Come in. Over."

Emma breathed a sigh of relief as she picked up the walkie-talkie. "Michelle. Where the hell have you guys been? Over."

"Our car hit something and we had to turn off to find a tire. The walkie-talkie wouldn't connect. Where are you?"

"Still on the highway. Where do we meet you?" Emma answered.

As they worked out our next location, my eyes remained fixed on Dan. I waited for him to turn around, acknowledge us in the back seat, but he didn't look back.

Sam's hand gripped mine, pulling my attention away.

"Bri? You okay?" she whispered, her eyes swimming with concern.

"I—I'm okay, Sammy." I tried to force a smile to ease her worry, but her expression remained unchanged.

I knew there was more she wanted to say. Hell, I had a whole slew of thoughts in my own head begging for release, but it was getting harder to know where and when to set them free.

When we finally reunited with the other car, we were pulled right into a lecture on safety and preservation. I wasn't surprised. Cap had made it very clear that we had to be conservative with the resources we had left, and we'd gone and given away far too much of what we'd had on hand to complete strangers.

Still, if given the choice, I'd do it all over again. And I had a feeling everyone else would, too. Even Cap, if they had been there.

Ultimately, it wasn't the fact that we'd given away supplies that was worrying them, but, rather, that most of the houses and stores we'd come across had been picked clean. We knew the day would come when we wouldn't be able to readily find supplies in abandoned homes or stores. Even canned food had to expire eventually.

There was an upside, though. With the lack of humans and technology messing with the world, that joke about "nature finally healing" was actually kind of true. The joke might have been a bit morbid now, but still.

The last few days we'd been shifting our strategy to finding what we needed in the wild. Forest Soup had made a comeback, and while I couldn't say I'd missed it, at least we knew how to get by on nature, for the most part. Did it slow down our progress? Yeah. But we were adapting, and that was something.

At least camping at night had gotten a bit easier. After high-heat days sweating in the humidity, even the slightest drop in temperature when the sun set felt like a gift. Evenings didn't just bring relief from the sun. The end of the day also meant we would finally reunite with the rest of our group in one spot. We'd have the freedom to talk about nothing or play low-effort games of "Who would win against a hell-creature?" or "Who would star on a celebrity apocalypse dating show?"

Okay, so the latter was a game that only Gabriela, Sam, and I played, but it was the time together that really mattered. For most of us, at least.

More often than not, when we'd all gather as a group at the end of the day, Emma would end up wandering off, distancing herself from the rest of us. At first, Dan and Michelle split the effort of making sure that Emma was never left alone for too long. But the last few days, Dan had taken on the role almost entirely. While she'd never admit it, Emma needed someone to just be there. And Dan was the perfect person, whether to have some company in silence, or a shoulder to lean on while he listened. I should know—he'd been that person for me since we'd met. But right now, Emma needed someone more than I did.

That evening, we'd opted to spend the night by a small body of water. It was just wide enough to provide a solid barrier at our backs, an obstacle to prevent people or wildlife from sneaking up on us too easily. The others had set up blankets on the ground or taken to sleeping in the cars. And tonight, Dan and I finally had some time to catch up, just us, thanks to a night-watch shift.

If only I could find a way to break the silence.

After the millionth glance out of the corner of my eye, trying to figure out what to say to spark up some conversation, I finally resorted to an old classic.

"Think it's going to rain anytime soon?"

"Maybe," Dan responded.

"It hasn't rained since murder-pig night."

My comment was met with a head nod, and I swallowed my disappointment as our conversation fell, dead on arrival.

Okay, so talking about the weather wasn't the most intriguing topic, but for some reason, I kept coming up empty. Though he was sitting just beside me, it felt like he was a million miles away. The distance between us had gotten to the point where even small talk about the weather was hard to maintain. I wasn't used to this dynamic—whatever it was.

My thoughts turned to the conversation I'd had with Carter during one of our last nights at the state park. He was someone I was used to sharing silence with—someone I'd ended up confiding in more than once because of the space he'd left open. He was like Dan in that way.

With Carter and Jason on their own, I had to wonder whether they'd found that middle ground yet. They hadn't left on good terms with each other, but then again, we had all been in a pretty shitty spot when we'd parted. I wondered how they were managing.

It wasn't like Jason was oblivious to what had started to spark between Carter and Alina. If anything, murder-pig night had only highlighted what we'd guessed at—there was something there, and neither Carter nor Alina were able to hide it.

Before I realized it, I was speaking my thoughts out loud.

"Think that was when it started?"

"When what started?" Dan finally looked over at me.

I sat up just a bit straighter, eager to keep him talking. "Carter and Alina. You know. Murder-pig night."

"Back on that again?" Dan laughed.

I smirked. "As if I ever stopped?"

Dan's head tilted slightly as he stared up at the night sky, thinking. "By that night, he was already down bad." He turned to me with a laugh. "Remember how he all but interrogated Sam about what you both saw when you woke up Alina that first day in the park?"

I stifled a laugh at the memory of Sam and Russell's retelling of the conversation.

"I'm telling you. Carter caught feelings. He's simping so hard, I almost feel bad for the guy." Russell cackled, gleefully reveling in the gossip.

The four of us were taking a break apart from the rest of the group, lounging in the truck bed in a small spot of shade.

"Don't laugh!" Sam scolded, smacking Russell's shoulder. "This could be good for him!"

"Yeah but what about J?" Dan added. "Lee could run him over, and he'd say 'thank you' and ask for more. Plus, Red said Lee's been in love with him since they were kids."

"Also facts," Russell agreed.

"Except Emma would never actually let them get together. You see how territorial she is with Alina," I countered.

Dan shook his head. "Nah, Red's chilled out on all of that. She's here for it now."

"Okay, fine, but what if Alina's moving on? She was legit blushing when she woke up next to Carter that day. Plus, Carter's got that whole mysterious, rugged survivor thing working for him. Not to mention, he's risked his life to protect her no less than three times already? Faced two hell-creatures and a murder-pig! Talk about knight-in-shining-armor vibes. You see the way they are around each other. There's totally something there—on both sides."

"Okay, but if we're talking about something being there on both sides, 'best friend's brother' is also hot," Sam added.

"Whose side are you on, again?" I teased.

A devilish smile curved across Sam's lips. "I mean, why not both?"

Russell's eyes widened. "Hold up, babe, be so for real right now. Does that mean—"

"Russ, if you value your life, do not finish that sentence," I interrupted.

"It's a good point, though," Dan mused.

Sam raised an eyebrow. "Which point?"

"Relationships are a social construct and society is just different now."

"So we're getting anthropological?" I teased, bumping my shoulder against Dan's.

"Just facts." Dan grinned as he leaned against the wall of the truck's bed, stretching his arm across the edge.

I settled back, the warmth from his skin grazing the back of my shoulders. From across the truck bed, I caught Sam's eye and she smirked.

"Well, there's something to be said about being able to recognize what's right in front of you, right Bri?" Sam glanced at Dan, a subtle move, one she knew only I would notice.

I laughed under my breath, shaking my head.

That was a debate best saved for another day.

"You ever think about what would have happened if we'd stayed?" Dan asked.

"Every damn day," I responded quietly. "We really had something good there."

The double meaning of my statement wasn't lost on me. It was as close as I could get to admitting the truth out loud. Whether Dan realized or not, he didn't say anything.

But he must have picked up on something, as he shifted closer, resting his arm across my shoulders. I leaned my head against him, not realizing how much I needed the comfort that came with his touch until that moment.

"We'll get it back someday," he said. "After all of this, we'll find it again."

SEPTEMBER 10, 2025

"Brian, come help me with this?" Cap called from across our camp.

"Sure thing!" I announced as I jogged over.

Sander was helping Cap wipe down our lone galvanized tub, and bottles of water lay scattered around their workspace. We'd stopped by another body of water to up our drinking supply and clean what needed cleaning, but now that everything was boiled and all of our bottles were filled, it was time to head out again.

"Do you mind helping Sander finish up here? I just remembered another spot we should check out—it used to be a wilderness school. I think it's along our route, but it's so hard to remember. I need to talk it out with Michelle."

Sander perked up. "Was it, like, an alternative school for kids or somethin'? I had a friend who was homeschooled and she told me 'bout how her parents sent her to this class a few times a week with other homeschooled kids. They got to garden and shit instead of sittin' through math. I asked my dad to let me do it, but he said it wasn't '*real school*.'"

Cap laughed gently. "No, not quite like that. There were some courses for younger folks, but it was mostly for people to learn how to live out in the wild—building shelters, finding food, navigating using natural landmarks—that kind of thing. They'd lead all kinds of expeditions, ranging from a weekend to months at a time, just focused on living in nature."

"I wish I got to learn 'bout this kinda stuff before the invasion. My dad and I used to camp sometimes, but it was always in one of those places with, like, a general store and cabins."

"Well, it's never too late to learn. And I have to say, Sander, you're a gifted learner." Cap beamed.

Sander's cheeks flushed as a bashful smile crept across his face from the praise, and I couldn't help grinning.

Sander had come a long way with our group since we'd smuggled him out of The Community. Though I'd had my doubts at first, the more time I spent with him, the more I found myself genuinely liking the guy.

While Russell had been trying to take Sander under his wing, it was crystal clear who Sander's true hero was. He took every opportunity to shadow Cap, enthusiastically asking questions and soaking up all the knowledge he could.

At first, I'd thought Sander's eagerness was because he was trying to prove he was on our side. But it was deeper than that. Each time someone recognized his efforts or asked for his thoughts, his walls came down just a bit more. From what he'd said about his time in The Community, I knew that he had often been overlooked, pushed to the side, ignored. Hell, it was the whole reason he'd been able to get away with working for the resistance while Willa had shacked up with the doctor.

One of the first things Cap had told Sander and Gabriela was that they had choices—that they mattered. Each passing day, we showed them that it wasn't just words; and in return, they showed us just how much they had to offer.

And it wasn't just Sander who was benefitting from Cap's newfound mentorship, either.

Though Cap didn't talk much about how they felt outwardly, there were subtle shifts that I'd come to recognize, hinting at the feelings they kept just below the surface. A hesitation in answering objections, re-checking plans to look for holes, the way they leaned just a bit more on Michelle than they'd used to. If I didn't know them so well, it'd be easy to overlook. But I knew them—knew *everyone* in our group—well enough to tell when they were struggling.

There was loss, and there was change, but there were new beginnings, too. And the more Sander came out of his shell, the way he leaned into Cap's guidance, I could see how the new friendship was healing both of them, even if it came in small, slow steps.

Just as Sander and I were wrapping up our task, a shriek tore through the gentle calm that had fallen around us.

Sander shot to attention, his eyes wide. "That was Gab!"

My heart pounded as my focus snapped to where Gabriela had been working with Emma and Dan. Three people had approached Emma, Dan, and Gabriela, and a tall white man with a thick, muscular build had his hands on Gabriela's shoulders as she struggled to break away.

"Get Cap and Michelle!" I ordered Sander before racing toward the trio of strangers surrounding my friends.

Just as I reached them, Emma pulled back her fist, slamming it into the jaw of the man who had grabbed Gabriela. He staggered back, rubbing the point of impact, temporarily stunned. The other two people with him flinched, but thankfully didn't make a move to return the attack.

"Don't fucking touch her!" Emma snarled at him as Dan tried to hold her back.

"Crazy-ass cunt hit me," he growled, bending down to pick up a broken metal pole lying next to what I assumed was his discarded backpack.

He clenched his fist around the metal as his cold gray eyes narrowed in her direction. His face was all hard angles, fresh sunburn painting his forehead and cheekbones. As he squeezed the pole in his hands, the muscles in his shoulders tensed, as if he was fighting to hold himself back.

I froze. I hadn't thought to grab anything to defend my friends with in my moment of panic as I'd rushed over. The only weapons we had were Emma's fists and unbridled fury.

"Stop, Frank! Put that thing down!" the woman behind him urged, before shooting a panicked look toward us. Her dark eyes were wide with worry as she raised her shaking hands, trying to show she wasn't a threat. The woman's tan skin was covered in old scrapes and bruises, hinting at the struggles they must have faced on the road.

"I'm sorry. I'm so sorry!" she whimpered.

I eyed the trio, but aside from Frank, the other two kept back. Their faces were heavy with exhaustion, their clothes wrinkled and dirty from what looked like multiple days of wear. As my eyes shifted to the third member of their party, I couldn't ignore the sickly, greenish hue that flushed across his face. He looked like he was about to pass out or throw up—maybe both.

He took a step forward, wincing from the movement, but it wasn't us he approached. Instead, he faced the man who was still holding the makeshift weapon in his grip. "Come on, Frank. Put it down. You're scaring them."

Gabriela cowered behind Emma and Dan, shaking uncontrollably as her tattoo pulsed with bright bioluminescent light against her pale skin. Her entire body was practically glowing from the intensity of her mark.

"Everyone needs to take a step back," I finally choked out, moving in front of my friends, attempting to create a barrier. I might not have been that great in a fight, but at the very least I could try to slow Frank down if he chose to come after us. Hopefully. Maybe? Fuck, I was *not* prepared to handle this.

But at least for now, Frank wasn't advancing. He kept his eyes fixed on Gabriela. The more his travel companions pushed, the more his expression seemed to morph from frustration into anger. I didn't know exactly what the group wanted from us, but I had a sinking feeling that whatever it was, it had to do with her.

"If that creepy fuck doesn't take his eyes off of her, I'll claw them out and shove them down his *fucking* throat!" Emma thundered, jabbing her finger toward Frank.

Her ice-blue eyes were burning with rage as she pulled against Dan's hold, trying to get at the man who refused to back down. Before anyone could say anything further, a gunshot erupted, the explosive sound stealing all of my senses.

I nearly choked on my own breath, whipping around to check my friends. Gabriela was huddled between Russell and Sam. In the chaos, I hadn't even noticed they'd arrived. Russell caught my eye and his jaw tensed. I could tell he was struggling to hold himself back—but with both Sam and Gabriela attached to him, he would stay by their side, for now.

Just in front of them, Dan had his arms protectively wrapped around Emma as they crouched on the ground, his eyes darting around, frantically searching for the source of the gunshot. His eyes met mine for a moment, and the panic eased just slightly as we assessed each other. I wanted to go to him, but my feet were cemented to the ground as my pulse pounded in my throat.

As the remaining three members of our camp approached, I realized it was Michelle who had fired the warning shot. Cap and Sander were close behind her, their own guns still aimed at the interlopers.

Michelle rushed to my side, grabbing my arm and assessing me quickly. My heart was pounding so hard, I could barely take a full breath around the invisible rock that had lodged in my throat. It took me a moment to register that she was speaking to me.

"We're here. You're okay." I finally processed her words as she gripped my arm, squeezing just hard enough to bring me back to reality.

I nodded, shaking myself out of the shock as she protectively pushed me behind her. Michelle took a step forward, aiming her weapon alongside Cap and Sander, who were standing deathly still with their own guns raised.

"Put your weapon down, or the next shot won't be a warning!" Cap threatened, their voice cold and commanding as they focused on Frank.

"I swear—fuck, I'm sorry! We just—her mark! I promise we aren't trying to—" The woman fell to her knees with her hands raised in the air, quaking from head to toe. The weaker-looking man sank to the ground next to her, and Frank finally threw the jagged pole to the side, shooting a disgusted look at his two companions.

"I just wanted to ask her some questions," the larger man stated as he kneeled next to the other two, his voice *too* calm.

"You don't grab a girl if you *just* want to ask questions," Russell snapped from behind us.

"It's a simple misunderstanding." Frank locked eyes with Russell. "You know how it can be."

"Nah, man. I don't think I do." Russell's eyes narrowed.

The fear in my chest turned into burning anger as Frank smirked in response.

"It's time for you to leave," Michelle jumped in, her voice firm. "Pick up your bags—*only* the bags—and back away."

Though Michelle spoke to all three of them, she kept her eyes on Frank.

His jaw worked as he ground his molars together, his eyes flitting back to Gabriela.

"Please—I'm sorry," the woman from their group called out. "We got off on the wrong foot, I know. I—my name is Elizabeth. This is Charlie. We just want to talk about the mark. It looks like ours."

"Except ours doesn't light up like that," Frank added in a gruff tone.

"You're marked too?" Michelle questioned warily.

"Yes!" The woman nodded emphatically, her short dark curls bobbing around her face. "We woke up in a school. There were others, but they were sick—like Charlie." She gestured to the less-threatening man next to her.

He coughed, leaving specks of blood on his lips. "We were laid out on tables. I thought I was in a morgue. Then I realized it was a cafeteria."

"Tables?" Gabriela asked, peering around Sam. "Not pods?"

Elizabeth's brow furrowed. "No. Just tables. Rows and rows of tables."

"Why don't you tell us your story, girl. What do you know about the mark?" Frank interrupted.

Gabriela opened her mouth to answer, but Cap spoke up before she could say another word. "The invaders put the mark on whoever they abducted. We don't know more than that. And like we said, it's time for y'all to go."

"Oh, come on now. We're just talking." Though he grinned as he said it, the look in his eyes was anything but friendly as he studied Cap from head to foot.

I *knew* that look—the judgment, the posturing. I'd been on the receiving end of stares like that enough times to know that even if he didn't threaten us with physical violence, this man was dangerous. The way his companions swapped worried looks as they quickly took a back seat to the growing confrontation only solidified my judgment.

We'd come across people like this before. In the past, we might have given them the benefit of the doubt for the sake of the other two. After all, sometimes you couldn't help who you were stuck with. But we weren't a large group anymore, and times had changed. As guilty as I felt sending away three people who needed help, it was too much of a risk to interact with them any longer than we had to—especially when all of the flags were bright-as-fuck red.

If there was one thing we'd learned, it was that danger wasn't always overt. Sometimes the most telltale signs were revealed in a lingering stare, or the opposite—who their eyes avoided, the voices they chose to disregard.

In the end, we gave them some of our water and a few pieces of jerky we'd been saving before directing them to the nearest town. It was better than nothing. Honestly, it was probably more than what others would have done for them—especially after such an aggressive interaction.

As the last of our bags were loaded back into the cars, I noticed that Dan and Emma had separated from the group. I heard their voices before I saw them, following the sound.

"I didn't know you could throw a punch like that, Red." Dan laughed under his breath.

"Yeah, well, that creepy fuck deserved it. Who grabs a girl like that?" Emma sniffed, taking in a shaking breath. "I thought he was going to take her. Just like—"

A heavy silence fell, and I was close enough now to see their silhouettes under the shade of a tree. Emma sank to the ground, leaning against the trunk, holding her head in her hands. Her shoulders started shaking, and as Dan knelt next to her, pulling her into his side, I couldn't help feeling like I was intruding.

"You stopped him. She's safe."

"But what if next time, I can't? What are we even doing? All of this —it feels like we're just driving in circles. We have a half-built radio that Cap can't figure out. We're low on supplies. The only people we're coming across are more fucked up than we are. And that's saying something. What if we never get them back?"

I swallowed hard, finally realizing why Emma had flown off the handle so hard. It wasn't just that Frank had grabbed Gabriela—I doubted she'd even seen Gabriela in that moment. It all came back to Alina. To Jason and Carter.

"We gotta take it one step at a time. We'll find a way. It's hard as hell, but I got you, Red. We're in this together. No matter what, I got you."

They fell silent, Dan's hand tracing slow, soothing circles over Emma's back as they huddled together against the tree. The comfortable way they'd settled against each other pulled a slew of emotions to the surface I wasn't quite sure I knew how to name. But it sure felt a lot like drowning.

Finally, I shook myself out of my thoughts long enough to make my presence known.

"Hey, Dan, Em. We're, ah—we're just about ready to head out."

Dan raised his head, nodding in acknowledgement. "Thanks, B. We'll meet you back there in a minute."

Emma shifted slowly, sighing heavily as she detangled herself from Dan's arms and pushed herself back up to standing.

"No, no it's fine. I'm fine. Let's just go."

Worry creased my forehead as the mask of calm indifference slid back over her features. She dusted bits of dried grass from the back of her legs before running her hands through her hair, shaking out the last of the tension she carried.

"You sure?" I asked as she walked toward me. "If you need a moment—"

"Nah—I can cry in the car just as easily as under a tree," she joked half-heartedly. She hesitated as she reached my side, searching my face. "Are *you* okay?"

I decided on a half truth, knowing that if I outwardly denied what

I was truly feeling, Emma would see straight through the bullshit. "Just getting over the adrenaline. It's nothing. I'm probably a little dehydrated on top of it. I'll grab some water in the car."

"No, you'll grab some water *now*." Emma linked her arm through mine, pulling me back toward the cars as if her conversation with Dan, the heavy emotion she had been caving under just seconds ago, was nothing. "Not going to have you passing out from heatstroke on my watch."

She didn't let go until we were back at the truck, and even then, only to grab a bottle of water and hand it to me. As I unscrewed the cap, she didn't take her eyes off of me.

"Bri, what's really going on?" she asked.

"You mean aside from another traumatic encounter with strangers?" I raised an eyebrow, hoping she'd take the hint and stop digging.

"Yeah—no, I know. That whole situation was... well, let's hope it's the last time we run into someone like *that*." She stared up at me, chewing on her bottom lip. "Are you sure there isn't something else on your mind?"

I shrugged.

She huffed a sigh, and I could tell that my non-answers were getting to her. I just wasn't in the mood to deep dive on all of the conflicting emotions running through my head.

"I guess I'm just worried about you," she continued. "You seem, I don't know, distant? You've been quieter lately. It isn't like you."

I'd confided in Emma enough in the past for her to be able to tell when something else was going on in my head. But I wasn't exactly comfortable opening up to her just yet. And of all times for her to be asking, why now? It felt like there was something she wasn't saying—an answer she was looking for. What was she hoping to find?

I spoke slowly, trying not to let my frustration show. "Emma... where is this coming from?"

She hesitated.

I was right. There *was* something else.

"I told you. We're just worried—"

Her statement hit like a punch to the gut, and I didn't wait for her to finish before interrupting, "Whoa, wait—*we?*"

Emma cursed under her breath. "Ugh, I knew I was going to mess this up. Listen. It isn't my place to say, so I'm *really* trying to respect that, but Dan's mentioned some things—"

The words tumbled out of her mouth like white water rapids crashing over rocks as she tried to explain herself without actually saying anything. I couldn't follow what she was talking about, let alone understand why she was bringing anything up at all.

"Emma, really?" I interrupted, heat rising in my chest. "Distant? I'm still *here. I* haven't gone anywhere. I haven't changed. So, whatever this is, you can stop digging. And, if what I just saw was any indication, I'm assuming *Dan* is the other half of your 'we?' If Dan is so concerned, why isn't he just talking to me himself?"

"Question of the motherfucking century," Emma mumbled. "Brian, I'm not trying to play a game of fucking telephone—I really just wanted to check in with you. I'm just—UGH! I can't get my words right!"

She grabbed my hands in hers, looking up at me with crystal-blue eyes that hinted at all of the conflicting emotions she was trying to keep under the surface. "Listen, I don't have some hidden motive. I don't want to force you to talk, but clearly there is something going on and *I see you*, Bri. And I know I haven't been around like I should be. Ever since Alina—" Her breath hitched, and she took a second to compose herself before continuing, "I just want you to know that no matter what's going on, I'm still here for you."

I was half tempted to break down there on the spot and pour out all of the thoughts I'd been holding on to. But it didn't escape me that it was Emma who'd confronted me—not Dan. And she was still part of the reason why I felt this way, even if it wasn't her fault.

But Emma was my friend, too, and I didn't want to just throw that away. She was here, and she was trying.

I took a breath, gathering my thoughts. "It's just been—"

"Yo, you guys ready?" Russell interrupted before I could say another word.

Emma practically growled in frustration. "No! We were *talking*, Russell. Did you not see that we were talking?"

"Hey, Emma, it's okay." I forced a smile.

Her eyes darted back to Russell for a moment before looking back at me in concern. I held out my arms for a hug, a peace offering. She pulled me in, squeezing me tightly around my ribs.

As I started to let my arms slip away, releasing her from the embrace, Emma didn't let go. She kept her hands laced behind my back, holding me close as she stared up at me. "This conversation isn't over." She gave me a stern look. Her voice softened as she continued, "I love you, Bri. And I *am* here. Always. No matter what. I hope you know that."

I forced another smile as I responded, "Of course. Love you too, Em."

Russell threw his arms around our shoulders, pointedly looking between the two of us as he added, "And Russell loves both of you as well, but it's time to peace out before more sketchy-ass randos find us."

SEPTEMBER 14, 2025

"THIS lead will actually pan out?" Sam asked as she trod over the ungodly amount of popcorn kernels covering the floor as if they were tiny landmines. I'd nearly slipped three times already as we tried to make it to the concession stand.

Russell, Sander, and Gabriela were outside picking through cars in the parking lot. It hadn't taken much convincing for Russell and the teens to believe that the movie theater would be a valid place to look for supplies while the other half of our camp was at a gas station down the street. Though, Sam and I had ulterior motives for stopping here.

It was a small theater—only four screens, an office, two bathrooms, and a tiny projection room—so it wasn't hard to clear, just a quick perimeter sweep. And a bonus? The place still smelled like popcorn. The whole experience brought to life such nostalgia, I couldn't help but feel giddy.

Dan's birthday was in just a few days, so when I spotted the little movie theater in the town we were driving through, I knew I had to make this pit stop happen. After my conversation with Emma, I'd tried to grab time alone with Dan to talk. But he'd suddenly become the king of excuses, quickly finding ways to avoid hanging out in any capacity. And considering we were a camp of nine people literally stuck with each other twenty-four seven, that level of avoidance was hard to pull off.

And Emma had the nerve to call *me* distant?

Still, even though I wasn't quite sure where Dan and I stood, if I didn't try and make something happen for Dan's birthday, I'd regret it. Don't ask me why it mattered so much—it just did. And thankfully Sam was more than happy to be part of the secret plan.

"Well, even if the next location's a bust, at least we'll hopefully get some good snacks out of this pit stop." I gestured to the counter in front of us where colorful bags of sweet and salty treats sat waiting behind glass.

"Dan is going to absolutely lose his mind when he sees what we found." Sam laughed. She hopped up on the counter, swinging her legs over to the other side. "It'll be a good pick-me-up for the others, too."

After the electronics store, it felt like much of our progress had stalled. While Cap had been able to find most of the essentials needed to build the anarchist radio, they were having trouble figuring out how to put it all together in a way that actually *worked*. And without the radio, we had to rely on luck to track down anyone who could help us.

Lately it had felt like we were trying to find our way while blindfolded and bound. Our mission to track down people who could actually help us kept leaving us even more skeptical of anyone we came across—especially after our last encounter with the former abductees.

"Okay so I see the stuff inside this case, but that can't be all that's left, right? Where do you think the rest of the candy and stuff is? Do we take popcorn with us? Oh! Maybe they have nachos! Or pretzel bites! Man, the things I'd do for some pretzel bites," Sam rambled with joy as she kneeled beside the counter, digging out the bags of candy from the glass display case. Her happiness was contagious, and I found myself buzzing with giddiness right alongside her.

"I worked in a movie theater like this once," I stated, grinning at the memory. "I was a projectionist. Our theater was small like this one and we kept the extra stock locked in the office. We should still search the cabinets behind the concession stand, though. Even if it's just napkins, cups, and popcorn buckets—we can definitely use them."

"I miss the movies," Sam replied wistfully. "The second we figure out how to power whole buildings again, I demand a movie night."

I laughed, heading toward the theater's small box office. Overall, things felt lighter today, and I decided to take it as a good omen. As I spotted the unopened boxes of candy and snacks stacked in the back of the small room, I couldn't help feeling like our luck was about to change.

"Jack-fucking-pot!" I cheered.

"You found it?!" Sam yelled, the tile echoing with the slap of her sneakers as she ran to meet me.

I turned around with a grin as her footsteps reached the doorway to the office, but any joy I'd felt was immediately replaced with cold fear as my eyes met hers.

At first, I thought the hulking shadow was a trick of the light. Before I could blink, he was on her with a curved blade pressed to the delicate skin of her throat.

Sam's mouth opened in a silent scream as the blood drained from her face. Her sparkling brown eyes were all pupil as undiluted terror chilled the warmth I was so used to finding in her stare.

The corded muscles of his arm were the first thing I processed. He had to have been holding her small wrists in one hand, from the way Sam's arms were wrenched behind her back. His other forearm was pressed against her neck, the curved blade just touching the racing pulse of her carotid artery. From the way the blade glinted, it looked sharp enough that even the slightest pressure would slice through her skin without effort.

His face was hidden beneath the brim of a tan cowboy hat, casting shadows over his features, but I could just make out the thin curve of his mouth, wrinkle lines worn deep in ochre skin, and the salt-and-pepper stubble lining his angular jaw.

Fear coated my body like a cold sweat as he drawled, "I don't make a habit of cuttin' up little girls, and I don't want to start today."

His voice shook my senses free, and I finally choked out, "Please!

Don't hurt her. Please, please let her go. I swear I'll do anything! Just—"

"Do you have weapons?" His voice was low and steady, calm. The duality of his soothing tone and the weapon he kept at Sam's throat was beyond unnerving.

"Yes," I whispered. "Pocketknife in my back pocket. Hunting knife in my backpack."

Sam whimpered, her eyes widening as she tried to wordlessly communicate with me. I knew she'd be telling me to run if she could have gotten the words out.

I'd rather die than leave her.

"Turn around and take out the knife. Throw it to the side. Then sit on the ground with your hands behind your head. As long as you keep listenin', we won't have any problems."

I threw the knife to his feet and sank to the ground, lacing my fingers behind my head. The others were still outside, and I could only hope curiosity didn't get the better of them. It was enough that I'd put Sam in danger. How could I have been so careless? We hadn't been gone long, so hopefully time stayed on our side—as long as the others remained where they were, hopefully he'd just let us go.

"Alright, miss, I see your knife stickin' out of your back pocket. Any other weapons on you?"

"N—no," Sam whimpered.

"I'm gonna let your hands go so you can take that knife and drop it to the ground. Then you can sit with your friend. Y'all are doin' just fine." He spoke gently, coaxing her to move slowly. As soon as her knife hit the ground, true to his word, he removed the curved blade from her neck.

Sam all but collapsed as she scrambled to my side, choking on a sob. I pulled her against me, holding her tight as I stared up at the man in the doorway. He took a step into the room, pausing to pick up my discarded pocketknife, and the light from the office window pushed away the shadows obscuring his features.

He was older, with lines hinting at his age crinkling the corners of his light brown eyes. Aside from his cowboy hat, he was dressed simply—a white T-shirt, jeans, hiking boots. That is, if you didn't count the arsenal that covered his body from head to foot.

The curved blade in his hand was nothing compared to the machete strapped to his side. In addition to the handgun in a holster on his hip, he had a rifle on his back and a pair of nunchaku clipped to his belt. His boots had slots for smaller knives, and I was sure there were even more weapons that weren't as visible.

Maybe I was scared past the point of reason, but there was something about the expression on his face, the tone of his voice, that made me want to give him the benefit of the doubt.

"I locked the doors so the kids outside won't be gettin' in too easily. Like I said, I don't want to hurt anybody. Just tryin' to be safe. Name's Laurence, but my friends call me Laurie. What's your story?"

"I'm... I'm Brian. We're just trying to get supplies."

"Clever idea, checkin' out the theater. You won't find much from the five major food groups, but supplies are supplies," he affirmed, crossing the room in two long strides to grab my backpack.

Silence fell over us as he dug through the backpack with one hand, keeping his eyes on us the whole time. All I could do was hold on to Sam and wait. At least this guy didn't seem like he wanted to hurt us. Hell, if he did, we'd have probably been dead four times over, judging by the number of weapons he carried.

"Is it just the five of y'all?" Laurence asked.

"No," Sam responded. "There are more of us, not even a mile away. So you should probably let us go before—"

"Patience, girly. I'll let you go soon," Laurence answered before Sam could finish. "Just had to make sure you weren't an immediate threat. As long as you keep playin' nice, we won't have any problems. Hopefully y'all learned a lesson in basic safety, at the very least. Don't you know how to secure a building before you go pokin' around? You never know what you'll find these days—you have to stay vigilant."

If it were coming from anyone else, the message might have been condescending, but there seemed to be genuine concern laced in his words. Sam relaxed against me, and I found my guard dropping as well.

"Where did you come from?" I asked, curiosity getting the better of me. "We checked the whole theater and there wasn't any sign of anyone."

An amused smirk curved across his mouth as he watched us. "You missed the hatch leading up to the roof in the projection room."

"Are you from around here, Laurence? Do you have people nearby, too?" I asked, wanting to learn more about the guy.

"Oh, I'm from everywhere and nowhere. Here and there. Just me, myself, and I."

I didn't miss the way his lip twitched, as if he were holding back a laugh.

Laurence's eyes narrowed in thought as if he were having some internal debate. Finally, he asked, "Y'all hungry? I'm not but an hour from here, and I got some vegetables from my garden that'll be too far past ripe to eat if they aren't cooked today."

"Wait, seriously? You just had me at knifepoint and now you're inviting us to dinner?" Sam asked.

"Don't take it personal." Laurence shrugged. His focus shifted to the window overlooking the parking lot, and as his eyes widened. Voice dropping in awe, he added, "Besides, if we're judging by the company we keep..."

I followed his gaze, and my heart skipped a beat as I realized the rest of our group had come back. Not only that—Cap and Michelle were making their way toward the theater.

The racing of my pulse picked right up where it had left off as soon as Sam tensed in my arms. We were just getting to calmer ground—if he saw them as a threat? My eyes shot to Laurence to gauge his reaction, but he was . . . smiling?

He moved quickly toward the door, unlocking it before bursting through, his voice booming as he called out, "Copernicus! And... Michelle? Well aren't you a sight for sore eyes! I shoulda known I'd be runnin' into you two eventually!"

"Did he just—does he know Cap and Michelle?!" Sam exclaimed.

"Laurie?!" Michelle's voice echoed through the lobby, and that was all the confirmation we needed.

We scrambled to our feet to follow Laurence, taking in the unexpected reunion. Laurence shook Cap's hand vigorously before taking Michelle's and kissing her knuckles. As the three exchanged greetings, I caught sight of Dan from across the parking lot. He was leaning against the back of the pickup next to Russell, who was speaking animatedly, likely speculating about the ninja-cowboy who was laughing and joking with Cap and Michelle like they were old friends.

Sam and I reached Laurence's side, and it took a moment for Cap and Michelle to register our presence.

"So, I'm guessin' these young folks belong to you?" Laurence drawled, pulling out our pocketknives and my hunting knife.

I reached to take them back, but Laurence leveled me with a look that said, *Don't even think about it*, before he passed the blades to Cap instead.

"I'd expect better from two kids traveling with *the* bushcraft expert, Copernicus. You'll get those back when you earn 'em," he directed toward myself and Sam.

"Laurie, you are exactly the same as I remember you." Cap laughed—actually *cackled*, completely overlooking the fact that this strange man had clearly disarmed us.

For a moment, I thought we'd escaped a potential lecture in safety, but one look at Michelle's stern expression changed my mind.

"Have we taught you two nothing?" Michelle snapped before pursing her lips. "You're lucky it was Laurie you ran into! After everything we've gone through—"

"Aw, Chelly, let's save the lecture for later," Laurence teased. "Besides, I'm sure they learned a lesson they won't soon forget."

Michelle glared at him, and I swear, the intimidatingly tall ninja-cowboy actually flinched.

The others had made their way over, and the expressions crossing their faces ranged from intrigue to skepticism.

Emma sized Laurence up, taking stock of each weapon on his body as she crossed her arms over her chest.

"So, how exactly do you know Cap and Michelle?" she asked. I didn't miss the way her eyes narrowed in assessment before flitting over to scan Sam and me to make sure we were both truly in one piece. Out of everyone, she seemed the least willing to trust Laurence.

Cap tilted their head in thought. "It was through Darryl, right? He had that friend Lucinda who introduced us to Leo who set up the whole bushcraft retreat that year."

Laurie nodded. "After the bushcraft expedition, we kept in touch through snail mail for years. Copernicus was a bit of a legend in our circle. I learned a lot from them."

"You're one to talk." Cap raised an eyebrow at Laurence. "This guy has a fully self-sustaining homestead off-grid. He's even built his own weapons."

"Holy shit," Russell exclaimed, snapping his attention to the tall man at our side. "Man, if you've been off-grid, do you even know what's been happening out here?" A solemn look crossed his face as he rubbed the back of his neck. "Dude. I hate to be the one to tell you this, but the world pretty much ended. It was aliens—"

"Oh dear Lord, Russell. Please just stop talking," Emma groaned at the same time Dan asked Russell, "You do realize off-grid doesn't mean underground, right?"

Finding Laurence was a shot in the dark, but one that actually hit its target.

For the last two weeks, we'd been driving around central Texas following a rough map of locations where we might find help, from what Cap could recall from their connections to bushcraft enthusiasts, survivalist groups, and off-grid preppers. If there was anyone who would be willing to help our cause, we figured people who already had a passion for fighting the interference of corrupt governing entities—of which, The Community would definitely qualify—would be our best bet. Though getting our friends back was at the heart of our mission, we couldn't forget that the greater purpose of our efforts was to stop the alien-worshipping cult from spreading.

And we had finally found someone we could not only trust, but who had the means to help us work toward that goal. Laurie was more than happy to lend us the tools we needed to get our anarchist radio functioning. He even offered to gift us some of his handmade firearms.

Laurence wasn't at all who I had initially expected. For someone carrying more weapons than he had fingers, he was surprisingly gentle and soft-spoken. By the time we all agreed to take him up on his offer for dinner and follow him back to his place, even Emma's skepticism seemed to have relaxed. There was just something about him.

Laurence—well, Laurie, as he insisted we call him—had ten acres of property in the middle of nowhere. And "middle of nowhere" was not an exaggeration. The drive to Laurie's home could have been the start of a classic eighties slasher flick—that is, until we actually arrived at Laurie's place. His property was a literal dream brought to life.

Every inch of land had purpose. From the flowering plants, fruit trees, and gardens to the water collection bins to the solar-powered generators humming behind the house—Laurie's home was a literal oasis.

The inside of Laurie's home was even better. Warm, soothing scents of leather and vanilla greeted my senses, followed by the gentle herbal undertones of the planters lining each windowsill. Gingham curtains framed the front windows of the log-cabin style house, while plush, cushy area rugs beckoned us to rest on comfy corduroy couches set on their perimeter. But it was the kitchen that was truly magical.

Pothos climbed the curtain rods around each window, with little herb planters of thyme, mint, sage, lavender, and chamomile lining the sills. As I peered out the window above the sink, I noticed a patch of corn plants, a large square garden with what looked like a bunch of different root vegetables, and a generous piece of the backyard dedicated purely to tomatoes. Beyond the gardens, I could just make out beehives, as well.

I turned in a circle, admiring the quietness of the space we'd begun settling into without a second thought. I couldn't remember the last time I'd felt so at peace.

"Is this actually real life, right now?" Russell sank into the couch and pulled Sam down with him. Gabriela and Sander plopped down on the other side, taking in the space with awe.

Laurie beamed. "Make yourselves at home. There are only three bedrooms, but I think I have some air mattresses around here somewhere. The couches are small, but I'm sure some of you might find them comfortable for the night."

Though he seemed to live alone, he didn't come across as a "loner." Especially considering the way he had welcomed us with open arms, so willing to share what he had. I wondered if maybe he had family somewhere, or whether we could expect anyone else to be popping in. He didn't have any pictures up, or many decorations at all aside from what was functional.

"Thank you, Laurie," Cap said. "This is... honestly, I don't even have words."

"I know we have to talk shop, but y'all should take a load off and rest a while. I'll get us a nice meal goin'."

"I'm not a good cook, but I don't mind helpin' if you need it," Sander volunteered, as Gabriela nodded emphatically from beside him.

Laurie chuckled. "Thank you for the offer. The best way y'all can help is by getting some rest. Feel free to wander. You'll be safe here as long as you stay on the property."

Everyone else fell into casual conversation, asking Laurie questions about his homestead as he worked in the kitchen. But I found myself unable to focus, suddenly overtaken with restless energy. So, I slipped outside, tilting my face to the sun.

As the warm rays kissed my cheeks, a sleepy sort of calm wrapped around my body. This was exactly what I'd needed. Lazily, I strolled through the yard, stopping to check out the vegetables and flowers that had managed to thrive here.

Chickens clucked in their pen as a dove cooed from up in one of the fruit trees, and their quiet songs melted the remaining tension from my body. What must it be like to exist in such tranquility all the time? The garden was alive with sound, brimming with life, and I soaked it all in.

I couldn't help wondering whether we could build a life like this one day. If, after we got Alina, Jason, and Carter back, we could all settle down in peace somewhere. Being here, it felt like it could actually be possible. And who knew? Maybe it wasn't just wishful thinking. Threads of optimism strengthened in my chest, weaving back the strands of hope that I'd thought had been lost in the weeks we'd spent searching for help. Maybe this was when it would all turn around.

I sank down onto a rocking bench that I suspected Laurie might have made himself, when I realized I wasn't alone anymore.

Michelle was strolling across the yard, a calm smile on her face as her cheeks turned pink from the sun.

"Oh! Hey, Chelle," I greeted her as she strolled across the grass.

She beamed, giving a lazy wave.

I scooted over on the bench, making room for her to sit next to me.

Michelle settled against the back of the wooden frame, and as she exhaled, it was like any remaining stress she carried melted from her body.

"You know, I always wanted chickens," she said, matter-of-factly.

I chuckled, following her gaze to the pen across the yard. "Oh yeah?"

She kept her eyes fixed on the birds as they pecked at the ground. "Cap and I talked about building a coop in our yard at one point. We even went as far as to go see baby chicks at one of the farm stores. But the damn HOA." She shook her head. "Who knows. Maybe there are chickens in our future after all."

The corner of my mouth tipped into a smile as I replied, "I was just thinking the same thing. Maybe one day all of this could be something we build for ourselves." I gestured to the yard. "Think we could pull this off?"

"Oh, I know we could. Though, I think we'll need to work a bit on our teamwork and communication first." She raised her brows, leveling me with a serious expression. "What happened today? It isn't like you to act so recklessly. Was a pack of Sour Patch Kids really worth risking your life over? And why keep it secret like that? Did you really think you were going to smuggle forty boxes of candy out of the movie theater without anyone asking questions? You and Sam are supposed to be the responsible ones."

I winced as the guilt from earlier built back up, stronger than ever.

"I'm sorry. You're right," I replied softly. "It wasn't our best move. Would it make you feel better if I told you I had a really good reason for it?"

Michelle pursed her lips. "No, but try me."

"It was for Dan," I confessed. "It's his birthday in a few days. I just wanted to do something for him—for all of us. It sounds lame when I say it out loud, but..."

"Birthday." Michelle rolled the word off her tongue like it was something foreign. "I can't remember the last time I thought about something so... normal."

"It just felt important, you know? Like, if I could just get this one thing right, maybe it would turn everything else around. And I mean, in a way I guess it did work out—"

Michelle narrowed her eyes, but before she could resume her mandatory lecture, I quickly sputtered, "Which was an *incredible* amount of luck and karma that we'll likely *never* run into again, so I should *never* make such an ill-informed decision *ever* again but—everything has just felt so off since, well, you know."

Michelle sighed deeply, her expression softening. "Oh, trust me. I know. But while it worked out this time, we won't always get so lucky. There are only so many Lauries left in the world."

I gasped, eyes widening in mock surprise. "You mean there are *more* ninja-cowboys with off-grid secret oases out there?"

"You'd be surprised," Michelle deadpanned, and I couldn't hold back the laugh that burst free.

Her expression turned serious for a moment and she took my hand in hers. "You know I hate having to be the bad cop, and I promise this is the last of my lecturing. But I don't know what I'd do if anything else happened to *any* of you. You have to promise me you'll be more careful."

The look in her eyes, the concern, the familiar warmth of being cared for and having someone who loved me enough to be so angry I'd put myself in danger—it brought me right back to all the times my mom had given me the same kind of talks as a kid.

I swallowed the lump of emotion forming in my throat, barely able to form the words as I answered, "I promise. And... thank you, Michelle. My mom would be really happy to know I have you."

Michelle wrapped me in a tight hug, swiping away a stray tear. "Damn you," she whispered, breath hitching. "I came out here to yell at you and here you are making me cry."

I'd never asked her or Cap if they ever wanted kids, but somewhere along the way, they'd become more than just the leaders of our group. They were ours, and we were theirs. Forever.

Truth be told, we never really talked about the families we had lost. Most of the time, it hurt too much to dwell on. But right here, right now, all I could think about was how lucky I was. How I hoped that wherever my parents were, that they had someone loving them enough to look out for them, care for them the way my friends did with me.

SEPTEMBER 17, 2025

FOR THE FIRST time in months, I woke up actually feeling rested.

One of the perks of Laurie's off-grid sanctuary was the fact that he had solar-powered hunting cameras rigged up around his property with a live feed that could be monitored from his office. Not only that, he'd managed to set up an alarm system that alerted him when anything larger than a dog wandered through the property.

The first couple of nights, we still took our usual night-watch shifts from the comfort of Laurie's office. But last night, we decided to put our trust in his system. After all, he'd been surviving on his own for nearly ten months this way, and with far less incident than we had. And finally—without the pressure of traveling, scouting, scavenging, and foraging—we were able to actually get some solid rest. And what's more? *Actually* relax.

We hadn't planned on staying longer than one day, but as Cap and Michelle talked through our plan with Laurie, he'd managed to identify at least fifty reasons why we should take more time to regroup.

So, we stayed.

Laurie helped Cap figure out the last pieces needed to get our anarchist radio working, while Michelle and Sam used Laurie's long-range radio to connect with groups in range who Laurie had been staying in touch with. It would take time to build up trust and convince others to join us in fighting back against The Community, but at least we were able to spread the word in one place, for the time being. Things were moving forward, and a renewed sense of fight had begun to spark within our group.

While Laurie, Cap, Michelle, and Sam worked on the technical pieces, the rest of us had been tasked with taking on the other responsibilities necessary to keep Laurie's homestead in working condition. There was gardening, checking traps in the woods surrounding his property for game, processing the water from the water collection bins, taking care of the chickens, and other general maintenance that Laurie hadn't had the chance to get to with his focus on our radio.

Laurie's whole setup was beyond impressive. Not only could he completely live off of his own land, but he had a whole list of where to find harder-to-get resources—like oil that could be turned into diesel to power his backup generators. Turns out, that was why he had been at the movie theater to begin with. Who knew corn kernels and the junk left in oil traps could be so versatile?

Though most of our days had started with chores, today was different. I'd woken up at the crack of dawn with Sam, Russell, and Gabriela, and we'd spent the better part of the morning decorating the kitchen to surprise Dan for his birthday. Gabriela and Sam were in the middle of stringing up a handmade "Happy Birthday" sign while Russell and I stacked the boxes of candy we'd recovered from the movie theater into something more decorative in appearance. We were just about done when Sander strolled in, rubbing the sleep from his eyes.

"What the hell? You put all of this together this morning?" His eyes widened as he took everything in. "Is that a castle?"

Since we hadn't been able to keep the candy a secret, what with being disarmed and caught red-handed by Laurie, we'd had to get a bit more creative in surprising Dan for his birthday. Hence, candy-box castle.

"Sandman!" Russell cheered, just a bit too loudly. "Welcome to the pre-party!"

"Russell! Quiet! You'll wake up the others!" Gabriela hissed as her eyes darted to the hallway Sander had emerged from.

In order to keep the surprise a surprise, we'd had to find a way to seclude Dan in the farthest bedroom in the house. He was typically an early riser and a light sleeper, and Sander was the only one of us who slept quietly enough to act as a barrier between Dan and the rest of the house should Dan wake up too early. We'd convinced Dan that him taking the room with Sander last night was part of our attempt to rotate sleeping quarters to keep things fair. It wasn't too unusual— any time we wound up in a place where some sleep spaces were better than others, we'd sometimes draw straws or rotate who slept where so everyone could get an opportunity to take advantage of the comfier spots. I had no doubt Dan had known something else was going on, but thankfully he'd just accepted the arrangement for the night.

Russell threw his arm around Sander's shoulders, leading him over to our candy-box creation. "So, what do you think? It's legit, right?"

"It's... somethin'," Sander replied noncommittally. "Is there a spot for presents? I made this for Dan. It's nothin' special but—"

Sander held up a sheet of paper with something drawn on the front.

"Can I?" I asked, reaching out my hand.

A sheepish look crossed Sander's face as he nodded, passing the paper my way. "I know Dan likes to draw, and I used to do these comics sometimes when I got bored in school so I figured... I don't know."

On the piece of paper was a scene with four roughly drawn characters debating who would win in a fight—a kraken, Mothman, or Slenderman. As I looked closer, I realized the tiny details Sander had added to each character—it was us, the Twenty-Somethings. Sam's curls, my glasses, Dan's baseball hat, Russell's wild grin. In such a simple picture, he'd managed to capture the perfect amount of detail.

"This is great, San! Damn, I'm kind of jealous that I can't keep it."

Sam came to peer over my shoulder, and a wide grin formed on her face as she turned to Sander. "Sander! This is so sweet! Dan is going to love it."

She gave him a quick squeeze, and his cheeks turned pink as he mumbled his thanks.

"Oh! That reminds me! I should get the thing I made him!" Gabriela darted over to her backpack in the living room and dug out a small parcel. "It's a friendship bracelet. Kind of. I took pieces from clothes that had rips and tears and turned it into a little woven bracelet with bits collected from everyone! So he can always have a piece of all of us with him."

"You know, I was wondering why there was a weird hemline on my tank top after you helped out with laundry." Sam laughed. "This is seriously awesome."

"Shit!" Russell said. "I didn't know we were doing gifts. I didn't get him anything. Can I hop in on the candy credit? I mean, technically I *was* part of the mission."

Sam rolled her eyes in response. "You get credit for helping to build the castle."

Russell grabbed Sam by the hips, pulling her closer. "What would *extra* credit look like?"

Sam's eyes flicked to Russell's mouth as it curled into his signature lopsided grin, and she wound her arms around his waist. "What kind of extra credit are you looking for?" she asked.

Gabriela sighed next to me, a dreamy look crossing her face. "Can I have that? I want that. How do I find *that*?"

Sander groaned. "Not this again."

I laughed, bumping Sander's shoulder. "What, you aren't pining for your own post-apocalyptic love story?"

Sander's face went deadpan as he responded, "It's enough being surrounded by all of y'all twenty-four seven. I'm fine just focusing on survival, thanks."

Gabriela wrapped her arms around Sander's waist, leaning her head on his shoulder. "One day you'll see someone from across the rubble of our war-torn city, and that little black heart in your chest will grow three sizes bigger, and I'll be right there to say, '*I told you sooooooo.*'"

She giggled as Sander ruffled her hair, pushing her away. "That's all you, Gab."

The more I hung around Gabriela and Sander, the more I appreciated their friendship. While Gabriela was a bouncing ball of sunshine and rainbows, Sander was the exact opposite—humble snark and full of black-cat energy. They were yet another example of two people who would have likely never crossed paths in pre-invasion life, but had grown to be inseparable as friends.

"What about you, Brian?" Gabriela asked. "You're on my side, right? Team Love Story?"

"Do you even have to ask? I mean, it's kind of obvious, isn't it?" Sander jumped in, gesturing to everything in the room.

Because of course he'd pick that moment to highlight his superior observation skills.

Gabriela's eyes widened. "Wait, you mean—"

Heat creeped up the back of my neck and I did my best to look nonchalant as I frantically searched for the right response.

Luckily Sam interrupted, steering us all back on track.

"Okay! We have limited time, kids. Let's get back to work."

"*Kids?*" Russell said. "Real talk—I feel like you need at least five years on someone before you can call them 'kid.' Also, now I'm low-key really missing Carter. When we get him, Alina, and J-Man back we should throw them a welcome home party. Can you imagine the look on C-Dawg's face if we did something like this for him?" Russell grinned as the conversation shifted, but I didn't miss the sympathetic look he shot my way.

I nodded at Russell in thanks, knowing that he had kept the conversation moving for my sake. Because even if we never talked about it, Sander was right. It was *painfully* obvious how I felt. And at this point, I was pretty sure the only person who didn't know was Dan, himself—either from being gloriously oblivious, or willfully ignorant.

It wasn't that I was avoiding having the conversation with him— well, not entirely. I'd worked up the nerve a few times when I'd thought that maybe what I felt wasn't completely one-sided. But insecurity always got the better of me. Plus, he was my best friend, and I was more terrified of losing that than anything else. I could deal with unrequited feelings. But if anything were to ruin what we had as friends? I didn't know if I could come back from that.

So, I didn't talk about my feelings outwardly. Well, most of the time. Out of everyone in our group, I'd only ever gotten close to telling Sam and Emma the whole truth. I guess that's why everything was hitting so much harder, now. There was always a limit to keeping something bottled up inside before it all imploded, and every day I was getting closer to letting it all spill over.

But, for today at least, I was just happy to be able to do something for my friend.

We made quick work with the rest of the decorations, and just in time. It wasn't long before Emma, Cap, Michelle, and Laurie filtered in, adding little trinkets to the growing pile of gifts in front of the candy-box castle.

"I have to admit, this is lookin' pretty good," Laurie said as he surveyed his home, and he was right.

We'd used discarded pieces of cardboard, leftover paint, and twine to put together various hanging decorations in addition to the "Happy Birthday" sign and candy castle. The only thing we were missing was our guest of honor.

"So, who's going to wake Dan up?" Emma asked.

"I vote Brian," Sam called out, her lips quirking into a smile.

"Second that!" Russell quickly added.

I rolled my eyes. *Way to be subtle.*

"Alright," I agreed. "But you all have to hide and stay quiet. I really want this to be a surprise."

Excitement buzzed through my body as I made my way down the hall. I was determined to make this a good day for everyone—something we could hold on to when we were inevitably thrown back into the chaos that was the world outside of Laurie's safe haven.

Sander hadn't closed the door fully when he'd left the room earlier that morning. Quiet as we had tried to be, it was honestly a miracle Dan hadn't woken up sooner.

I stepped into the room, not bothering to be quiet. The trundle bed was still pulled out, with the blanket Sander had slept on rolled into a rumpled ball at the foot of the mattress. Dan slept on his side, facing the wall, and I could just make out the notebook he kept as his sketchpad clutched under his arm.

"Hey, Dan," I called out, not too loudly, as I didn't want to startle him. "Time to wake up, dude."

He groaned, shifting underneath the thin sheet draped across his waist. Rolling over, he yawned deeply, stretching his arms above his head before sinking back against his pillow, eyes still closed. He rolled his shoulder, the muscles in his bicep tensing as he sleepily bent an arm over his face. Clearly, he was not ready to get up just yet.

I moved over to the window and pulled back the curtains. Golden rays stretched across the room, highlighting his rich brown skin in soft morning light as he blinked awake.

His deep russet eyes met mine and in a raspy, sleepy voice he finally spoke. "Morning already?" He looked to the empty trundle bed and his brows raised in surprise. "Damn, I didn't even hear Sander get up. Dude is quiet as hell."

The corner of my lips tipped up as he rolled onto his stomach, hugging the pillow under his cheek.

"Looks like you slept well, then?" I asked.

"Deadass, best sleep I've gotten in a long time. Everyone else up?"

"Everyone but you. How's that for a change of pace?"

The corners of Dan's eyes crinkled as he grinned, and I couldn't help the smile that crept across my own face.

He reached his arm across the bed, grabbing his sketchbook and flipping through the pages. It was clear he was in no rush to get up. But considering the rest of our friends were currently hiding in Laurie's kitchen and living room, I had to speed things up a bit.

I crossed the room, straightening Sander's discarded blankets enough on the trundle so I could push it back underneath the full-sized bed Dan was still lying in. I hoped he'd get the hint and start moving, but instead he propped himself up on an elbow, watching.

As I stood back up, he shifted on the mattress, making space beside him. Dan gestured toward the spot with his sketchpad. "Want to see what I've been working on?"

I should have been convincing him to get up, but I couldn't resist the invitation. As I lowered to sit on the edge of the bed, he skimmed through the pages, finding the right one before passing his book to me.

Four silhouettes stood in a field facing a sunrise shaded in black and gray. There was just a touch of gold in the sky, the only flash of color on the whole image. I recognized the forms immediately—Dan, Russell, Sam, and me. Russell stood on one end, his arm wrapped around Sam, whose head was tilted against his shoulder. His other arm was raised in the air, as if he were emphatically gesturing along to a story he might have been telling. I could practically hear his voice, Dan had captured his essence so perfectly.

Dan had placed Sam in the middle, next to me, with her hand resting on a slender popped hip. Though her face wasn't visible, I knew the exact expression she would have been wearing—the amusement that would have been shining in her eyes. She stood confidently beside us, her stance strong, balanced, and so incredibly her.

My focus shifted to the way Dan had drawn me next. My elbow rested on Sam's shoulder, my body language suggesting someone completely at ease with himself. *Was that how he saw me?*

My arm was just touching Dan's in the drawing, leaning against him ever so slightly. Dan was the only one of us who wasn't facing forward. Instead, his head tilted to face the rest of us.

We were all connected through touch in the picture, the symbolism clearly representing our closeness in real life. I could practically feel the relaxed ease from the scene, and wished I could step inside of the drawing and fully sink into the moment he'd captured like a memory you could hold in your hand.

I let out a slow exhale. "Damn. It's pretty fucking perfect. I love everything about it."

Dan tilted his head to look at the drawing with me, his temple just resting against my arm. We sat like that for a breath longer before his hand brushed against mine to touch the page on the sketchbook.

"Thanks, B. Thought you'd like that one," he said softly, finally sitting upright as he took the book back.

His lips parted as if he were about to say something else, but before he could, Russell's voice echoed from down the hall, interrupting the moment.

"B-Man! D! You alive? We're all—ow!" There were muffled voices I couldn't make out, likely lecturing Russell for almost ruining the surprise—

Oh, shit. Right. Dan's surprise.

I jumped to my feet, grabbing Dan's arm and pulling him toward the door.

"We should probably see what that's all about," I stammered.

My heart pounded in my chest as I led him down the hall toward the connected living room and kitchen. Breathing deep, I tried to play it cool, counting down as the decorated room came into view.

Five, four, three, two...

"Happy Birthday!" a chorus of voices rang out as our friends jumped up.

"Oh, shit!" Dan exclaimed, and I grinned.

"That's today isn't it?" he added as his eyes scanned the room before finally landing on the candy-box castle at the center of the kitchen island. "Does this mean I can finally have some Sour Patch Kids and Swedish Fish? Did the M&M's make it?"

"Yeah, man. It's all there." I laughed.

"We got you other presents, too!" Gabriela cheered, bouncing from one foot to the other, unable to contain her own excitement.

Sam practically tackled Dan in a hug, kissing his cheek as she wished him "Happy birthday!" in an excited squeal.

Russell slapped Dan's hand in a high five before pulling him into a one-armed bro-hug, clapping him on the back for good measure. "Sorry I almost ruined it, dude. By the way, the candy castle was my idea."

Sam crossed her arms, glaring at Russell, but he pretended not to notice, grinning at me with a thumbs-up instead. I laughed, shaking my head, but didn't bother to correct the statement.

After well-wishes from Sander, Cap, Michelle, and Laurie, Dan turned to me, his eyes shining nearly as brightly as his smile. "You made all of this happen, didn't you?"

"You bet he did," Emma said from behind me, curling an arm

around my back as she beamed up at me. "Bri poured his whole damn heart into this one."

She squeezed me once more before reaching out to Dan, hugging him and pinching his cheeks. "One year closer to that frontal lobe being fully developed! You just might make it yet! Happy birthday, babe."

Dan snorted a laugh, wrapping his arms around Emma and murmuring a thank-you in her ear before letting go.

She winked before sauntering off to join Cap, Michelle, and Laurie, who were trying and failing to fend off the rest of the group from attacking the candy supply.

"Damn vultures," Dan joked, his voice low enough that only I would catch what he'd said.

I chuckled. "You should have seen them when we were setting up. I thought I'd have to get Laurie out here with his weapons stash just to make sure all of the treats lasted until you finally woke up."

Without warning, Dan wrapped his arms around my neck in a tight hug, catching me off guard. The warmth from his breath hit the shell of my ear as he murmured, "Thank you, B. This is everything."

My forehead pressed against his shoulder as I hugged him back, soaking in the moment.

SEPTEMBER 19, 2025

I SCANNED THE BACKYARD, looking for Sam.

We were getting ready to leave Laurie's house, and she'd mentioned wanting to take some time to write a letter to Carter before we hit the road again.

It was something she'd started doing after a recommendation from Michelle, not too long after we'd left Carter and Jason at the abandoned farm. Sam had always carried a journal with her, taking the time to document what we'd been experiencing whenever there was a moment to reflect.

I'd tried it once, penning my own letter to fill in Carter, Alina, and Jason on what we'd experienced the day after we'd run into Laurie. But as I'd read it back, I couldn't help feeling like I'd gotten the prompt wrong, messed up the facts. Writing might not have been for me, but at least it seemed to help Sam.

Except for today.

When I found her, she was sitting against the chicken coop, hugging her knees to her chest with her tattered journal abandoned at her side.

"Hey, Sammy, what's wrong?" I asked, crouching in front of her.

When she didn't answer, I moved to her side, wrapping an arm around her shoulders. She leaned in, hugging my waist as she buried her face against my chest. Tears bloomed, forming small wet pools that soaked into my shirt, and my heart squeezed, aching from the weight of her obvious pain.

"It's been nearly a month," she finally whispered. "I was sitting down to write a letter to Carter, like I always do, but when I looked at the dates—how has so much time passed already? What if he thinks we gave up on him and Jayce? What if Alina is—"

Sam couldn't finish the sentence. She didn't have to. My mind had followed the same trail many times before.

"I know. I know, Sammy."

I tried not to think about it too often. I'd realized early on that the more time I spent dwelling on what I couldn't control, the harder it was to *want* to go on. And we had to keep moving at all costs. One step at a time. One foot in front of the other. Following uncharted paths led by the hope that we'd find something better waiting for us somewhere.

That didn't mean any of us could help looking back. And like staring at the road behind us trailing in the rearview, sometimes the memories were closer than they actually appeared.

"I was thinking about what Gabriela said after her nightmare the other night," Sam whispered, pulling away so she could meet my eyes.

I tugged off my glasses, rubbing the lenses against my shirt, thinking back on the conversation we'd had with Sander and Gabriela after everyone else had gone to sleep.

Gabriela had woken up screaming again. It happened frequently, with varying degrees of terror. Sometimes it was like her body would wake up, but her mind would still be trapped in the nightmare, reliving the torture she'd experienced in the doctor's labs at The Community.

Willa had considered Gabriela her personal prize. But Gabriela wasn't the only Marked One Willa had kept locked away close. There were others. Like the little boy who was the feature of Gabriela's latest nightmare. The one she and Sander had been forced to leave behind.

"Do you think they're doing the same things to Alina? Keeping her locked up? The pain tests? The injections?" Sam asked.

Alina's face flashed behind my eyes. Her laugh, the optimism she carried like a shield. I thought back to the moment we'd met, how her first instinct had been to grab Carter and try to pull him down the street, away from the hell-creature that had been stalking her and Jason. Or the night we'd had to flee the safe house, when she'd lured another hell-creature away to give us all a chance to escape. I had no doubt that whatever The Community had in store for her, she wouldn't make it easy on them to keep her.

"Alina's a fighter. She'll find a way to survive," I said confidently.

Sam nodded, relaxing against my side.

"She will. They all will. They have to."

"Think Carter and Jason found a way to get along, yet?" I asked, changing the subject.

When we spoke about Alina, Carter, or Jason, we often reverted back to the debates we'd used to have at the state park. The way Alina had softened Carter's edges, the obvious tension between him and Jason, or even the awkward way Jason had pursued Alina—it had been like our form of reality TV, back then. In a way, bringing up their semi-love triangle now was a form of hope, too.

"You're really holding out for that bromance, aren't you?" Sam laughed, wiping the rest of her tears away. "Don't think I didn't read your letter."

"Hey, anything's possible, right?"

"In a perfect world," Sam said wistfully, her voice trailing off as she fell back into thought. "You and Dan seem better, by the way."

Since Dan's birthday, he'd started spending more time with us again. There was still some distance when it came to the two of us, but it was better than whatever had been happening in the weeks prior. Before I could find a witty way to brush it off, Sam started speaking again.

"Bri, it's me." She gave me a knowing look. "I think we passed the point of talking around the subject a long time ago."

Even without me saying anything directly, Sam had known for a while now how I felt about Dan. Hell, she'd probably seen it before I'd even admitted it to myself.

"I know," I quietly replied. "It's just . . . everything's been so weird the last couple of weeks. I don't know what to think."

"Sometimes I think *thinking* is your problem. Always too much going on in that head of yours." She smirked, tapping my forehead with her pointer finger.

"You *think*?" I joked.

"Brian," she groaned, laughing.

Sam leaned her head against my shoulder. I tilted my head against hers, reaching across my chest to hold her hand, finding quiet comfort in the contact.

That's one of the things I loved most about Sam. She always seemed to know when I just needed someone to be close. She knew me, and in that moment, the love I felt for her, her friendship, the way she cared in return, I could practically feel it wrapping around me, warm like the morning sun.

"You should tell him," she said gently.

I let go of her hand and picked a blade of grass, suddenly needing something to keep my hands busy. Tearing the blade of grass down the middle, I finally answered.

"I can't."

"But what if—"

"That's the problem, Sammy." I took a breath. "*What if*? I don't know if I'm ready to find out what's on the other side of that question."

"Even if it's happiness?"

I hesitated. "What if I'm scared of that, too?"

It wasn't long before the chickens came pecking at the ground behind us, clucking for their breakfast. After feeding them and gathering up some eggs, we made our way back inside where the others were already starting to pack up. Laurie leaned against the counter, watching us with a hint of melancholy on his face.

He thanked me as I set the eggs down, wrapping them in a tea towel.

"I'm going to miss the help around here, but I have to say, I'll miss the company even more," Laurie said. "This place never felt more like a home."

"That part was all you, Laurie," Cap replied, making their way over to the kitchen. "I can't thank you enough for all you've done for us. Welcoming us in, taking care of us, helping us get ready for this next part of our mission."

"Don't be so humble, Copernicus," Laurie chuckled. "I just provided the space. You and Michelle are the ones who made the rest happen. You found a good group with these folks. Don't know what I'll do when I wake up tomorrow to an empty house, only the chickens to keep me company."

"Wow, Laurie's laying the guilt on thick this morning. You really are going to miss us, aren't you?" Emma said as she hopped up onto the counter next to him.

"Maybe," he answered, his lip twitching into an amused smile. "I wouldn't be opposed if a few of y'all wanted to stay."

"We can come back though, right?" Gabriela asked, her voice light and hopeful.

"Or maybe you can come with us?" Sander added.

"And leave the chickens?!" Russell exclaimed.

"That's where your mind goes? The chickens?" Emma snorted a laugh.

"Are you kidding me? Bianca? Cheryl? Lynn? Bethany? Pablo? You can't just leave them here alone, Red. They can't fend for themselves. Half the time, they can't even tell their feed from a rock."

"Wait, the chickens have names?" Sander asked.

"Which one's Pablo?" Michelle demanded. "Last I checked, they were all chickens. No roosters."

"Pablo's a girl?!" Russell's brows shot up in shock.

"I can't believe this is the last conversation we're having in this house," Dan mumbled, shaking his head.

I caught his eye, and his lip quirked up in a half smile.

"Can't you though?" I asked.

"See, this is what I'll miss most. Y'all are somethin'," Laurie chuckled.

"Laurence—" Michelle held out her arms for a hug, and Laurie nearly lifted her off the ground as he hugged her back.

"I wish you could come with us," she said. "I hate the thought of leaving you here alone."

"I'm used to it. Plus, someone needs to keep talkin' to our contacts over the radio. With the work you and Sammy put in, I don't doubt you'll have some of 'em packin' up their bags to meet you down at that God-awful place to kick some ass. You'll have your army yet." He paused. "And Russell is right. My feathered ladies need me here."

"See?!" Russell exclaimed. "Laurie just gets it."

"I only have one request," Laurie said.

"Anything," Cap answered. "You name it, we got you."

"If you ever need a place to stay, even if it's ten years down the line —you come right back here. Alright?"

"Well goddamnit, Laurie. Now I'm crying." Emma sniffed, throwing her arms around his neck.

We took our turns saying goodbye. I knew I'd be feeling some type of way about leaving, but I hadn't expected all of the emotions to hit the way they did. When we'd met Laurie, I'd thought Sam and I were one breath away from meeting our untimely end. Instead, he'd saved us.

We'd only been here a week, and so much had changed. Throughout this journey, I was sure everyone had hit a point where they'd doubted whether we could actually pull off the plan, that we'd actually be able to get in contact with someone who could help—yet all it had taken was a chance encounter at an abandoned movie theater.

Hope struck in the most unlikely places. Call it destiny. Call it fate, luck, will of the gods—whatever it was, I had no doubt something greater had brought us together. More than that—from here on out, we had a real chance.

SEPTEMBER 23, 2025

"Is it too late to turn around and go back to Laurie's?" Emma grumbled.

We'd only been on the road for a few days, and some of us were taking it just a bit harder than others. After sleeping in actual beds, having a roof over our heads, and an abundance of real food at our disposal, going back to roughing it was... well... rough.

"I miss Pablo." Russell sighed, hugging Sam from behind and burying his face in her neck.

Sam patted his hands, holding back a bewildered expression as she replied, "Those birds really left a mark on you, huh?"

"Not gonna lie, I low-key miss them, too. They were like tiny, feathery dinosaurs," Dan added.

"Are they really talkin' about chickens? Or like, is that a metaphor for somethin'?" Sander asked in a hushed tone, shooting a confused look in my direction.

"I think they're really talking about chickens," Gabriela whispered back.

"Alright, I know you're feeling... feelings... But I want to run through the plan," Cap interjected. From the look on their face, they were struggling to find the right way to sympathize while keeping us on track. Since being back on the road and having to take up our usual night-watch routines, we'd all been having trouble adjusting to the broken sleep schedules. And it had left some of us a bit loopier than others. Thankfully, we had Cap for direction.

"Michelle, do you have the map?" they asked, looking to her for backup.

"Right here, my love," Michelle declared, spreading out the map on the tailgate of our truck.

The farther we traveled from Laurie's homestead, the more our little anarchist radio came in handy. It had taken a bit to get used to. Depending on how close we were to the next signal, it could sometimes take a day or longer for our message to transmit and receive a response. We'd finally gotten to an area with more reach, and responses were starting to pick up. There were three different groups interested in meeting with us and hearing us out. It was still a risk, but between the people Laurie had connected us with and the way word was spreading, we were closer than ever before to finding allies, and hopefully convincing them to join our mission.

"So, the plan is to meet up with the first group here." Cap pointed to a spot on the map. "We'll arrive before them and make sure we have an area with enough cover so we can watch them as they come in. Just because we have a connection, doesn't mean that the people we're meeting will be safe. Don't ever forget—this isn't the world it once was."

"Cap and I will be the ones to talk to them first. I don't want us putting our whole group in front of strangers in case things go sideways," Michelle added. "I trust that all of you will be able to follow protocol this time around?"

Though she spoke to all of us, she gave Sam and me a pointed look.

"Of course," I replied. "But I still think that you should let me go instead of at least one of you. You and Cap are the ones keeping this whole ship above water. If anything happens to you—"

"Everyone is important," Cap interrupted. "No one of us is more valuable than the other. Don't forget, I've trained every single one of you. I've seen how far you've come—everything you've learned. If something happened to me or Michelle, I know y'all would be just fine."

"Would we, though?" Russell answered warily.

"Yeah, Cap. You're giving us a *lot* of credit," Emma added.

"Sam's become an expert with the maps *and* the radios at this point," Cap said. "She probably knows more about troubleshooting the damn anarchist radio than I do. Dan and Brian are the best in our group at setting up traps for small game. And Emma—you have the most first-aid knowledge out of everyone. And when pressure hits, you know how to keep your focus, whether you believe in yourself or not. Sander is our best shot with a gun, and Gabriela's knowledge on foraging and finding edible plants has grown exponentially."

"And... what about Russell?" Russell asked tentatively.

Cap gave him a warm smile. "You aren't afraid to do the hard thing. You're an excellent judge of character and have really grown in being able to identify risks and knowing when to intervene. Don't think I didn't notice how you spoke to those guards that first day at The Community when Gabriela ran to Alina and Jason. You knew exactly what to say to keep them from reacting and give Gabriela more time. You made sure they didn't see us as a threat."

Russell grinned. "You caught that?"

To be honest, I hadn't even realized that was what Russell had been doing at the time, but thinking back on it now? The way he'd stepped in front of the rest of us, talking to the guards like nothing was wrong—he had been putting on a show. A damn convincing one.

When we'd stopped to help the man with the two kids, he'd done the same thing. His casually friendly demeanor was disarming in all the right ways, and somehow he knew just what to say to get someone to lower their guard.

"I still think you're giving us too much credit," Emma grumbled. But she didn't fight back further.

"I know what these groups can be like. They'll want a link to someone familiar, and with my connections I'll be able to convince them to at least hear us out," Cap responded.

"Plus, no one will look twice at the middle-aged, blond, white woman in tow. The bias will work in our favor. And with this little handgun hidden in my pocket, they'll never see me coming," Michelle added in a voice way too cheery for the threatening nature of her statement. She patted the gun she kept on her at all times for emphasis.

"Chelle, you're kind of scary sometimes," Emma replied.

"All the better to keep you safe, my dears," Michelle responded.

"Anyway—" Cap jumped back in. "For now, we'll set up camp here tonight. There's some good tree coverage and we can do some cleaning in that little river. Russell, Sam, Gabriela, and Sander, y'all can go do some light foraging while the rest of us get to work here."

The four of them didn't hesitate before trekking off into the trees, while the rest of us fell into our own tasks.

Cap and Michelle took dish duty, while Emma, Dan, and I scooped up our group's clothes and linens. For the most part, we relied on sun sterilization for cleaning clothes, but when we had the chance, it was always good to give everything a true refresh. It wasn't exactly my favorite chore, but it had to be done. There wasn't much that we had to clean, but we were trying to stay on top of it while we had the opportunity. The linens in particular were important, as we never knew when we'd need to use them to clean injuries. Plus, we were nearing *that* time of month where having extra linens on hand was about to be crucial. I made a mental note to put some extra chocolate aside when we took care of inventory later, knowing that Emma, Sam, and Gabriela would appreciate it when the time came.

"Are we sleeping in the cars tonight? Or are we setting up an actual camp?" Dan asked as we worked.

"I think we're sticking to the cars. Two people on watch, three people sleeping on the seats in each car, and even with the supplies packed away, there's enough room for the last person to squeeze into the truck bed," I answered.

"Hear that, Red? That's all you," Dan teased.

"Why?" she scoffed.

"Because you're short. You take up less room," he responded with a smirk.

Emma splashed water at him, sticking out her tongue. "Dick. I'm petite, but I'm not that much shorter than the rest of you."

"There's nothing to be ashamed of, you're just fun-sized."

I rolled my eyes, huffing under my breath as the two of them fell into their routine.

Emma glared at him. "You really need some new material."

"You telling me I need to aim higher? It might go over your head," Dan retorted.

Emma threw her hands in the air before turning to me with fake annoyance. "Bri, some help, here?"

I knew what she was doing. Ever since that awkward conversation the day we'd run into the former abductees, she'd been going out of her way to pull me into conversations with her and Dan to make me feel included.

I knew Emma felt bad about how our conversation had gone down that day. But at this point, clearly she had her own ideas of how to fix whatever our situation was, and I had no choice but to be part of her master plan. I debated calling her out on the interference, but then I had a better idea.

A grin slowly crept across my face. "Yeah, Dan. I gotta say, that was a *low* blow."

"There he is," Dan replied, eyes glittering with amusement.

"You assholes—" Emma exclaimed.

But once I got started on the puns, there was no stopping.

"Oh, come on, let's not get sidetracked by *little* details."

"Brian!" Emma growled, barely holding back a laugh.

"What can I say? It's just easier for some of us to rise to the occasion."

"*Brian!*" Emma practically screeched, launching herself at me. Dan clutched his stomach, laughing so hard he could hardly breathe, as Emma jumped onto my back in a sad attempt to tackle me to the ground.

"What are you doing?" I cackled. "Fricken spider monkey! Dan! Run! She's trying to get to a higher vantage point!"

"*Though she be but little, she is fierce,* motherfucker," Emma grunted, still trying to take me down.

"How are you quoting Shakespeare right now?!" Dan sputtered through his laughter.

Before anyone could say anything else, we were cut off by Russell's disembodied voice buzzing through the walkie-talkie.

"Base—come in."

"Oh, shit, we should get that," Dan said as he tried to catch his breath.

Emma hopped back down, bumping me with her hip and shooting me a grin. I looped my arm around her shoulders in truce, letting Dan pick up the walkie-talkie.

"We're here. Over."

"There's been a... development. Over."

Emma and I exchanged a puzzled look, before Dan responded again.

"Meaning? Over."

Russell answered after a beat, *"We're coming back, but before we do, I'm going to need you to promise not to panic."*

"Promise not to panic?!" Sam's voice repeated. *"Telling them not to panic will only make them think there's a reason to panic. Give me that!"*

Dan's brow furrowed as we waited for a response over the static.

"You've gotta be kidding me," Emma muttered, easing out from underneath my arm to grab the walkie-talkie from Dan's hand.

"Panic or not—tell us what the fuck is going on. Over," she ordered.

"Everything alright?" Cap called from where they were working with Michelle a few yards down. They shielded their eyes as they stared in our direction, waiting for an answer.

"Come here!" Emma waved them over as the walkie-talkie buzzed with static.

Then, finally, Sam stammered a response, *"We're safe. Everyone's safe. But we met some—well—"*

"What's going on?" Michelle asked as she and Cap approached.

"I don't know! They won't fucking spit it out," Emma snapped.

A cold chill settled through my body as anxiety seeped into my blood. We'd been in far too many compromising situations for a response that vague to *not* mean something more. Something was going on—and the longer we had to wait to find out, the worse my assumptions grew.

"I think you need to see this to believe it. We're coming back, but—fuck. I guess, yeah. Don't panic. Over," Sam responded.

Unshockingly, hearing the words, *"don't panic"* again did nothing to ease my nerves. I moved to Dan's side, standing shoulder to shoulder as we braced for whatever was headed our way.

But when I say there was nothing in this universe that could have prepared me for what happened next—

Like a scene from *Jurassic Park*, six giant hell-creatures emerged from the trees. They were larger than life, their bodies varying shades of gray, green, and brown—camouflaged to blend in with the forest. But as the sun hit their slinking forms, their stripes blinked to life. Their colors melted into blues deep as the sea, midnight navy, and shades of slate with glowing cerulean stripes. And my heart stopped in my chest.

Dan grabbed my arm, pulling me behind him as Michelle and Cap raised their guns. Emma scrambled to my side, eyes wide with fear, never once looking away from the aliens creeping ever so slowly toward us.

Each step was a long stretch, claws digging into the earth, but the creatures didn't move with the prowl of a predator on the hunt. A low rumble escaped the gaping jaws of one of the beasts, its rows of razor-sharp teeth gnashing. A slightly smaller creature released a series of clicks like an overly-caffeinated cicada. And that's when I realized that the creatures were accompanied by... people.

Our people.

And none other than Gabriela was perched on the top of the smallest creature at the rear of the group. But she wasn't the only one. There were others.

Dan's grip tightened on my arm as he pulled me closer. I was frozen—with shock or fear, I couldn't tell the difference.

Something moved behind the beasts, dashing between their legs to get ahead of the lumbering monsters.

It took me a moment to realize it was Russell, waving his hands in the air like he was signaling for us to stop.

"Don't shoot! We're fine. Everything's fine!" he yelled as he jogged over.

"What the fuck am I seeing right now?" Emma whispered through a shaky breath.

"Is that—are people riding the hell-creatures?" Michelle stumbled over her words.

Sander and Sam jogged after Russell, and the other hell-creatures with their riders fell back to allow Gabriela and her beast to head the group.

"Is that a glow behind their shoulders? Are they Marked Ones, too?" Cap wondered.

"It's okay!" Russell said as he approached us, panting. "They're safe."

"Safe? How is any of this *safe*?!" Emma snapped.

"Long story short—the bond that The Community was talking about? With their hell-creatures and the Marked Ones? The bond is real," Sam blurted out.

My eyes went wide as I realized what Sam was telling us.

The mind bond between a hell-creature and a Marked One—the connection that linked their minds with the alien beasts that The Community was trying to force on *all* of the Marked Ones they'd kidnapped—it wasn't just the ravings of The Community's sadistic doctor.

Because there was Gabriela, sitting on top of a hell-creature like it was no more than a fucking pony, her tattoo lit up like a halo around her small frame, pulsing in time to the glowing stripes of the alien monster that she was connected to.

Gabriela slid down the hell-creature's shoulder, an almost serene look on her face as she patted its leg. And the damn thing lowered its feline-like head to nuzzle against her cheek before she turned to us with a grin.

"There is *so* much I have to tell y'all."

Once we'd recovered enough from the initial shock, Gabriela filled us in on what had happened amidst the trees.

"And then it was like—I was inside the hell-creature's head. I could see her thoughts. Or something like that. We weren't communicating with words, but I just knew what she was trying to tell me."

The hell-creature Gabriela had bonded with lounged beside the rest of her group, along with the Marked Ones that they'd bonded with. All in all, there were six aliens and four Marked Ones.

I shot a look to where they rested by the trees. The hell-creatures were stretched out, or curled into each other, sleeping like lions in the shade. The people they were with kept to themselves, giving us the space we needed to hear Gabriela out.

Every instinct was still screaming to run, but the creatures weren't attacking. Nor were their people trying to advance. They were just sitting there, relaxed and waiting—as if they knew that we'd come around.

"I wish you could have been there to see it. There are no words," Sam said reverently.

"*I* thought we were going to die," Russell interjected. "We had one gun against a pack of hell-creatures. We should have been goners."

"Not. Helping." Sam elbowed him, giving him a stern look.

"Not gonna lie, if it were anyone but Gab tellin' us it was safe, I wouldn't have believed it either," Sander added.

"So, the bond is real," Cap said slowly. "But how do we know the creatures won't still attack?"

"The attacks weren't their fault," Gabriela replied. "The invaders have been torturing them, bringing them from planet to planet to fight all of these other predators like some kind of sick war game. They were scared. Every new place the invaders left them, they had to fight their way back to each other. The connection they have to us— the Marked Ones—it's like this irresistible pull. Once they feel the connection to a Marked One, all they sense is pain until they're able to reach the person calling to them."

Dan sat next to me, his whole body tense. He stared at the group of hell-creatures in the distance, his eyes cold, unblinking.

When the hell-creature had attacked our camp the day the invaders' ships had left Austin's airspace, he'd barely escaped with his life. The beast had left him with claw marks gashing his leg, deep enough that it had taken weeks for him to be able to walk without a limp. If Russell and I hadn't been there to distract the monster, there would have been little chance he'd still be with us today. It was a miracle he hadn't been injured more badly.

His grip was so tight around his scarred thigh, his knuckles paled.

I reached out, slipping my hand under his, easing his fingers from where they dug into his leg. He relaxed ever so slightly as he twined his fingers through mine, squeezing me instead.

"I got you," I murmured, low enough so only he could hear. "No matter what. I got you."

SEPTEMBER 29, 2025

PLANS HAD CHANGED.

Allowing the new Marked Ones and their bonded *companions* to join us was not a decision we made lightly. Hell, it was hardly a decision we made *civilly*.

Eleanor, the leader from the Marked One's group, and Cap argued for two days straight. Gabriela—of all people—ended up stuck in the middle as a mediator. Even with Sam, Russell, and Sander vouching for the band of hell-creature enthusiasts, insisting that if we'd been there, we'd understand why they weren't a threat— the truth was, we were too scarred to look at the aliens as anything other than monsters.

Eleanor was a tall, broad woman with platinum hair, and skin that was as pale as moonlight. When her tattoo lit up, she looked almost alien herself. The blue glow was so strong that the bioluminescent light almost seemed to pour from her whole body when her tattoo activated. She'd been the one to speak for the group and tell us their story, while the rest of the hell-creatures and Marked Ones hung back behind the tree line. They'd promised to keep their distance until we gave them the "okay," and they'd kept their word.

When we'd told them about The Community, all differences aside, they'd insisted on joining our mission.

At least *that* was a middle ground we both could agree on.

But it was Gabriela who had finally worn us down and convinced us to give them a true chance to help. Gabriela had the ability to sense the group's intentions through the bond with her hell-creature, who she'd adorably named Bitsy, since she was the smallest hell-creature in the group. From the way she'd described it, she could always feel Bitsy in the back of her mind. Bitsy was able to share memories as well, like a movie that played in Gabriela's head where she experienced whatever Bitsy had gone through as if she were living in Bitsy's body, experiencing it firsthand.

Apparently, the hell-creatures were all connected in a similar way. They had the ability to speak basic commands out loud through their growls, clicks, and trills, but any deeper conversation happened through that intimate connection. Not quite telepathy, but something more. Something deeper.

We'd also learned that Eleanor's group had woken up in a lab, much the way Gabriela, Alina, and Jason had described. Except when they'd come-to, it had been because the hell-creatures they were now bonded to had freed them. When the hell-creatures had clawed them out of the pods, they had been pulled into their bonds almost instantaneously.

According to their story, the creatures had sensed them, something almost magnetic, practically screaming for connection. They'd hunted the humans down, and upon finding the empty lab with the pods, clawed them out of imprisonment. From that point on, the creatures had cared for them like they were something precious.

What was most astonishing to me was just how different the experiences were for the groups of abductees we'd come across. Alina, Jason, and Gabriela had been abandoned in the city—their medical facility empty, with hardly any survivors. Frank's group seemed to have gotten the worst of it, with most of the survivors left incredibly ill. Then there was this group. They hardly seemed to remember anything about the facility itself, their strongest memories being that of their rescue.

The more we learned about whatever the invaders had done in those labs, the more questions we had about what their true goal was.

Clearly, the bond was a part of it—it *had* to be. From what we'd been able to piece together, it sounded like the tattoos were a means to call to the hell-creatures.

But the biggest question was still *why*?

From what Gabriela had told us of Bitsy's memories, the creatures were a means to an end—a way to wipe out whatever remained on the planets they invaded. So why the hell would they want what was essentially their war machines to bond with humans? Especially when, if this group's experience was to be taken at face value, the creatures seemed to want nothing more than to protect the humans they'd bonded to?

The bonded creatures hunted food for their humans, led them to water, and protected them from all kinds of dangers—from local wildlife to any people they'd crossed who'd shown any signs of wanting to harm their humans. Even now, if we moved too suddenly, we were met with shrieks and growls from the hell-creatures, who seemed constantly tuned in to what their humans were experiencing.

Ironically enough, it was their terrifying protectiveness that won over our trust in the end. Because clearly, if these people wanted us dead, their hell-creatures could have seen to it in a heartbeat. What's more, the creatures had come to our group's defense just the night before.

While Emma, Dan, and Michelle were on night watch, a mountain lion had snuck up on them. As the large wildcat tore from the trees, Bitsy and her big, glowing friends quickly circled Emma, Dan, and Michelle, creating a barrier against the mountain lion. Apprehensive as we were, we knew the extra protection would be in our favor, especially as we made plans to head back toward The Community.

That is, if we could manage to stay on the bonded humans' good side.

"So, what? Are we abandoning the people from the radio, now? After all of that work?" Emma asked in exasperation.

"No, not at all. We still need them. We're just going about it in a slightly different way because of our... company," Cap said, their eyes shifting to the patch of sun the hell-creatures had spread out across.

It was so strange seeing the giant aliens lounging around, docile as house cats, knowing the destruction they were capable of inflicting. They all had names, but the only one I bothered committing to memory was Bitsy. And only because she was part of Gabriela now.

"You should be thankful to have them," one of the Marked Ones, David, growled. His tattoo pulsed, the glow hovering like an aura over his tanned shoulders. His brown eyes darkened as he glared at Emma, who met his gaze with equal animosity.

In the distance, a hell-creature—likely David's, by the way it bared its teeth—poked its head up, eyes fixed on our group as a low growl rumbled from its chest.

"Tell that to the members of our group they slaughtered. Tell that to *Dan*, who is *still* recovering from what a hell-creature did to his leg," Emma shot back.

"Stop calling them hell-creatures. That's our kith you're talking about," another member of their group reprimanded. Molly. Her short auburn curls framed her heart-shaped face, giving her an almost cherubic look, even as her green eyes sparked with anger. She was my age, in her late twenties. Out of the four Marked Ones, she was the quietest, but like the others, she drew the line at any hell-creature slander.

It was the main point of contention for our groups at this point.

I wanted to see things from their perspective, but it was hard to push aside our own lived experiences.

"I'm sorry—" Cap intervened, shooting a look at Emma to back down. "We're trying, we really are. But you have to understand that what our group went through was beyond traumatic. We'll try harder to be careful with our words."

"You aren't the one who owes an apology," the last member of their group, the oldest, Sharice, stated. She was in her sixties, a veteran, and walked with a cane, having lost her leg during her time in service. She was the one who had insisted we accept their help, having known prisoners of war, herself. Sharice sympathized with our mission to get Alina back, to free any other Marked Ones being held at The Community. Though she didn't share much of her story, it was a reminder that underneath everything, we all had our reasons for fighting for humanity's survival. That war, trauma, and human-on-human violence was a constant cycle of destruction, and at least for the thirteen of us, we had the common goal of seeing it come to an end.

Hell, even the six extra-terrestrials who'd joined our party could relate to an extent, too.

Emma took a breath, and I could tell she was physically trying to restrain herself from arguing further as she gritted out. "I apologize. I didn't mean to offend you. I'll try not to let my emotions get the better of me next time."

"Now was that so damn hard?" David chided.

"Don't be condescending," Eleanor bit back. "We aren't going to get anywhere if we keep fighting like this."

"Respect goes both ways," Sharice added.

David swallowed hard, like he was choking down the rest of his argument as he mumbled an apology of his own.

"The people we've been talking to want to help, but they're still apprehensive, understandably," Cap explained. "But they have resources, weapons, and knowledge, all of which we need. They'll be crucial for whatever comes after our Community rescue mission.

"When I gave Carter and Jason their map, I told them to set up their base at a hunting lodge just far enough away from The Community to hopefully stay off their radar. So, that's where I'm directing those we've been in contact with."

"It's as good a plan as any," Eleanor said. "Our kith have been sensing their kind closer than before. The rest of the kith we've been tracking shouldn't be too far from here, and once we get them on board, we should be able to get your friend and any others out of that place. We'll have the numbers to hopefully force them into waving their flags instead of trying to fight."

"You underestimate the will of those who think they're working for a higher purpose," Sharice interjected. "If they believe in this *doctor* and his supremacy plans, there's no telling how far they'll go. We have to prepare for that."

"Of course," Cap agreed. "And we'll plan for that, too."

"Is this really happening?" Sam asked, a hopeful look in her eyes. "We're going to find Carter and Jason? Get Alina back?"

"It's happening," Michelle confirmed. "We're going back and we're going to get them all."

"My brother—" Emma whispered. "I get to see my brother again? I get to tell Alina—" Her blue eyes swam with tears, her shoulders shaking with the buildup as her voice hitched on a sob.

Dan pulled her in close as she all but collapsed when the realization hit, murmuring something in her ear that I couldn't make out.

"Let's motherfuckin' goooooooo!" Russell cheered, jumping up from where he'd been sitting on the ground, grabbing my shoulders and shaking until I couldn't help grinning back from his enthusiasm.

I met Dan's eyes from across the circle, a ripple of warmth fluttering in my chest as his mouth tipped into a smile.

This was it. We were ready.

The hell-creatures screeched, bounding toward us, and I tried to fight the terror shaking through my system as I ran alongside Dan to join our group where they'd gathered, looking out across the wide field.

Just as we'd been getting ready to hit the road, a bloodcurdling howl halted us in our tracks.

"Is everyone here?" Cap asked. They had a tight hold on Michelle's hand as they scanned our faces, quickly glancing at the hell-creatures and their bonded who had formed a tight circle around us. "Who are we missing?"

I skidded to a stop, scanning the faces of our group, but my brain was on overdrive and I kept losing count.

All of a sudden, Dan blurted out, "Red! We're missing Red! She was just here—where did she go?"

Gabriela gasped, her voice a low whine as she whimpered, "No, no, no..."

Michelle shot a look at Gabriela. "No panicking. Remember what we've been practicing. Deep breaths."

"Someone's approaching!" David called back to us, tensing as he stepped closer to his hell-creature.

I frantically looked around, trying to spot any sign of Emma, but she was nowhere in sight.

Gabriela gasped, and Sander grabbed her hands, stepping in front of her to try and keep her attention on him. Her eyes were glazed over as she connected to Bitsy, focused on whatever her bonded creature was communicating to her.

"No. It can't be!" Gabriela whispered.

"What do you see?" Sander asked.

"It's—how?" Gabriela shook herself out of the trance, and her mouth opened in shock for a second before she jerked away from Sander, running as fast as she could toward Bitsy.

The creature crouched down as Gabriela climbed onto her back, and before I could process what was happening, they were racing across the field.

"Gabriela!" Sander yelled.

My eyes shot to him just as he was about to take off running, and I grabbed him, wrapping my arms tightly around his chest.

"Stop! We need to stay together!" I protested as he fought against my hold.

Before he could argue back, a scream tore across the field, echoing from the trees in the distance.

My eyes shot to the tree line as my blood ran cold. I knew that voice.

It was Emma. Emma was screaming, and Gabriela had run off after her.

I shot a look at Eleanor's group and their bonded creatures to find that they were talking urgently amongst each other, gesturing toward the tree line, but staying put. Why weren't they moving? Why weren't they following Gabriela?

Something moved in my peripheral, and before I had time to process, Russell's voice frantically called out, "Sammy!"

And before anyone could react, he was racing after her.

"Fuck!" Cap cursed, before snapping at the rest of us, "Stay where you are. No one else moves until we know what's happening! *Goddamnit!*"

I shot a look at Dan, who seemed like it was taking everything in him to follow Cap's orders. Keeping one arm around Sander's chest, holding him against me, I reached out with the other to grab Dan's wrist.

"Don't go," I pleaded. We needed to stay together. Already, we were too scattered, and it would be harder to protect each other.

Dan nodded, stepping closer to my side as another scream echoed through the trees.

I turned just in time to see Russell grab Sam, pulling her to the ground. They scrambled over to a patch of taller grass, crouching low, and I hoped it was enough to keep them out of sight.

From the snapping branches, the pounding steps that echoed across the field, whatever was coming was nearly here.

With all of my focus on that, I almost missed Molly's voice as she called back to us, "You can relax! In fact, get out your damn party hats. I believe we're about to cross a name off of your list of people to rescue."

No sooner did she finish her statement, a hell-creature burst through the trees carrying two people on its back, followed by Bitsy and Gabriela.

"No fucking way," Dan exclaimed next to me as realization struck us both at the same time. We exchanged wide-eyed looks.

Michelle gasped, and I released my hold on Sander as we all recognized who had entered the clearing.

It was Jason.

"So, we made it to the hunting lodge, and turns out that's where the resistance had set up their base. One of the guards, Marc, was acting as a double agent," Jason explained.

He'd given us the abridged version of his journey with Carter—

who had volunteered to be taken into The Community. The hope was that he could help carry out the rest of the resistance's mission from the inside, while also ensuring at least one of them was with Alina.

I studied Jason, taking in all of the subtle changes. He and Carter had been struggling through their journey, running into setback after setback on their way to the hunting lodge. Though he glossed over most of the details, it sounded like he'd been in dire condition before bonding with *Gorte*—or, as he'd taken to calling the hell-creatures, his Octerra. He'd spoken about her in the same, almost reverent way, that the other bonded Marked Ones in our group had, urging the rest of us to adopt the phrase.

"*Marc*? You don't mean Marcus, do you?" Sander asked. "*That fuckin' asshole?*"

"You know him?" Jason turned to Sander.

"Know him? He's one of the fuckin' Sovereign," Sander replied with a bitterness I'd only witnessed when he'd spoken about the doctor. "Everyone knows not to cross him. If he's involved, it usually means you're about to be carted off and never seen again."

"Well, that makes sense," Jason said under his breath. He scoffed, shaking his head before continuing, "He brought people back from The Community. The two guards who helped us all escape that night? Kevin and Nathan? Everyone in The Community thinks they're dead, but they've been at the lodge ever since, helping run things there. You really didn't know about him?"

Sander shook his head. "Kevin and Nate were the only people in the resistance I had contact with. Figured there was more. I never knew who all was involved—none of us did. Makes a hellova lot of sense now, though. Fuckin' Marcus."

"Did he say what they were doing with Alina?" Gabriela asked, unable to hide the worry from her tone. "Is she okay?"

"He never really gave us much detail other than that she's alive and giving them hell."

"That's my motherfuckin' girl," Emma said, a sad smile on her face. "Thank goodness she's okay."

Emma clung to Jason's arm so hard, it had to have hurt. Though, if it did, he didn't make any move to free himself. He must have been just as relieved to be reunited with Emma as she was, him.

"So, Carter is in there right now with Alina," Sam stated, staring at Jason, studying his reaction. "But he's safe?"

"Yeah." Jason's Adam's apple bobbed in his throat as he swallowed. "Yeah, he's with her. Marc said he'd keep them together as much as he could. They're both as safe as they can be, given the situation."

"Damn, J-man, you got some balls," Russell said, eyes wide with astonishment. "You've been out on your own, just you and Gorte, gathering up hell-creatures left and right and building a goddamn army. You're the fucking GOAT."

Jason chuckled, shooting an appreciative grin Russell's way. "Man, I missed you guys. It's really, really good to see your faces."

After hours of catching up, introducing Jason to the other Marked Ones, and watching Gorte and Bitsy scamper through the field like rabbits hopped up on a mountain of sugar, we'd finally started winding down for the night.

Our plan was coming together better than we could have ever hoped for. With the addition of the Octerras and riders Jason had managed to recruit and send toward the lodge, we had more than enough people and extraterrestrials on our side to take down the Community and fully execute our plan.

After hearing Jason's recap on how he and Gorte had come together, I was also starting to believe that what Gabriela and Eleanor had said about the hell-creatures was true. They weren't innocent, but they were also victims in a much bigger story—one that we had only begun to scratch the surface of.

The way Jason described his bond with Gorte was so similar to how Eleanor's group and Gabriela described their own alien bonds, that I couldn't help but start to accept their stories. I had to give Russell credit for his *"You can't make this shit up"* logic when he had been arguing on their behalf. Eleanor's group's explanation, Gabriela's story, and Jason's details aligned. I doubted I'd ever be able to fully forgive the Octerras for what their kind had done to our camp, but shockingly, I was actually starting to trust them.

Plus, we had a common enemy.

Or, I should say, enemies.

There was one piece to the hell-creatures' history that kept tugging at the back of my mind. A piece that we hadn't fully talked about out loud, but I knew we'd have to face eventually.

On every other planet the Octerras had been sent to, the invaders had always come back to collect.

I had a feeling that we'd soon have to face the reality that the initial invasion had only been Phase One, and that soon, we'd have to start planning for their inevitable return.

But hopefully any other threats would wait. We needed to keep our focus on The Community—our next battle. And more than that, I needed my brain to stop going rogue so I could actually get some sleep and prepare for what lay ahead.

Everyone else had broken off into smaller groups as we turned in for the night. With seven Octerra at our backs, and both Gabriela and Jason urging us to trust them, the rest of the group had finally decided to give them a chance. Plus, we desperately needed to build our strength for the next leg of our journey.

At the time, it had seemed like a good idea to take the truck's bed for the night, but as I tossed and turned, I just couldn't find a comfortable position. Hours passed, and I found that no matter how hard I tried, sleep was nowhere to be found.

I sat on the tailgate, scanning our group, visually checking in on everyone.

Eleanor's crew slept soundly, close to their Octerra, who were all awake and alert as they watched over us. Just as they'd promised.

Most of my group had abandoned sleeping in the cars to camp outside for the night. The ground was dry enough, and with a few blankets to protect against the scratchy grass, there was more space to sleep comfortably.

Russell, Sam, Sander, and Gabriela had decided to sleep near

Bitsy and Gorte, who were dutifully guarding them. The creatures lay like sphynxes, their blue stripes glowing in the dark, a soft aura that lit up the area just enough to see my friends' sleeping forms clearly. As I made eye contact with Gorte, she let out a soft trill, almost like a purr.

Out of all of the hell-creatures I'd come into contact with, she was the one who made me want to believe that everything the Marked Ones said was true. There was just something about her—she had this weird little personality that made her seem more like a giant puppy than a menacing predator. As if reading my mind, she rolled onto her back, stretching all eight legs in the air with a huff before nipping at Bitsy's toes playfully, and I couldn't help smiling.

My gaze traveled to the spot where Emma and Dan had decided to sleep for the night. Emma was curled next to Dan, her forehead pressed against his shoulder as they both slept, and a familiar sinking feeling settled in the pit of my stomach.

On one hand, the way Emma constantly tried to pull me into conversations with her and Dan had me believing that she was truly trying to help bridge the gap between Dan and me. But seeing them so close, I couldn't help wondering whether the reason he'd continued to be so distant was because there really was something more between them—even if it *was* one-sided on his part.

I just couldn't bring myself to ask.

A twig snapped, and I followed the sound to the riverbed. As it turned out, I wasn't the only one having trouble sleeping.

I watched Jason as he moved to sit on the grass, leaning back on his elbows and tilting his head up toward the sky.

Earlier that evening, I'd found him in that exact same spot, taking a break from the rest of the group and all of the questions we'd been bombarding him with since he'd returned. Still, he'd welcomed me over, then.

He and Emma were similar in a lot of ways—they were siblings, so that was to be expected. But, really, he was more like Alina than his sister. Their openness, the way they both wore their hearts on their sleeves—it was so easy to be around them both. There was just something about him that made me want to open up and share everything. He felt safe.

Just earlier, I'd been on the verge of pouring my heart out about everything that had been going on with Dan. He must have known that there was more than what I had been saying out loud, because at the end of our conversation, he'd told me that if I ever wanted to talk, he was there. And he'd meant it.

Before I knew it, I found myself walking right back down to the riverbed, ready to interrupt his quiet space for the second time that evening.

He peered over his shoulder as I approached, greeting me with a half-smile. "Can't sleep either?"

I sat beside him with a heavy sigh. "Honestly, I don't know how *anyone* is asleep right now. After the day we've had? I feel like my brain's been on overdrive trying to process it all."

"Yeah, that sounds about right. I still can't believe I actually found you all again. Talk about sheer luck."

"What's really wild is that the Octerras in Eleanor's group are the first we've actually come across since splitting with you and Carter. Like, what are the chances that just as we find them, you find us?"

Jason ran a hand through his hair as he glanced over at Gorte, who seemed to be patrolling our camp's perimeter. Her large head cocked to the side as her ears tilted, funneling in sounds out of our human range of hearing. She trilled as she saw Jason watching and his eyes glazed over the same way Gabriela's did when she was communicating with Bitsy. After a moment, he nodded at Gorte, and she turned, trotting toward the tree line.

He faced me again, his amused smile turning into a more serious expression as he said, "I told you how I had two weeks to get as many Octerras on our side as I could, right? One week to travel, one week to return?"

I nodded.

"I'm not sure how much you learned about where the Octerras came from, but they're social creatures, like us. They have families, with connections so deep that it hurts them to be separated for too long."

"Yeah, Gab mentioned something like that."

"That pins-and-needles feeling that Alina, Gabriela, and I would get when an Octerra was close? That was the bond calling out. Once Gorte and I connected, it mostly went away. But the closer we get to the larger groups of Octerras, it starts coming back—just a little. But for Gorte? The other Octerras? They're feeling that pull from the moment they land on a new planet. Because even though they were sent here to destroy us—or humans without the tattoos, at least—more than anything, they just want to find each other."

"So you've been following that? The pull?"

Jason nodded. "Each group of Octerras we found would tell us the same story—that they were following the signs to a larger herd. But the last group we crossed? The story changed. Because more and more Octerras started heading toward The Community. We'd managed to find enough Octerras to keep word spreading about how we needed help. I was nearly ready to turn around and go back because we'd accomplished what we'd set out to do. But the last group we came across? One of them sent Gorte a memory from one of the Octerras in *this* group. From Bitsy. And I saw you all. It's how I found you."

I let out a sharp exhale, impressed at the lengths Jason had gone through, and that his journey had brought him right back to us in the end.

"Man, you are a frickin' badass, J. You really made all of that happen."

A grin slowly formed on his face. "Yeah, I really did, didn't I?"

"Not gonna lie, when you told us you volunteered for this instead of going for Alina, I was kind of surprised. I mean, the day we split up, you were ready to steal our only working vehicle to go after her."

Jason winced. "Yeah, not my best move. I just couldn't think, you know? But in the end, the only thing that matters is getting her back. It doesn't matter who's the one to physically do it, as long as we get her out."

"And you're not at all worried about Carter? And... her?" The words were out of my mouth before I could stop myself.

"I've had time to think—especially since Gorte and I started this whole adventure." Jason paused, a sad smile pulling at the corners of his mouth. "I love Alina. More than anything. I've loved her for a long, long time. And I didn't do anything about it until the invaders came."

"I mean, better late than never, though, right?"

"Well, that's the problem."

I frowned. "What do you mean?"

"Before Alina and I were abducted, we were in her apartment together, just the two of us. It was the most time we'd ever spent alone together, and in those moments—the ones I remember, at least—I finally was able to see what it could be like if we were really, truly together. And I mean—not ideal circumstances. Half the time, we were panicking over what was going on outside those apartment walls. But..." he trailed off, letting out a deep sigh. "My memories have been coming back in pieces—more since I bonded with Gorte. It's like our connection opened up these dark spots in my mind, and slowly all of these moments I lost are fading back in. There's this one memory, just her and I. And every time I close my eyes, it's all I can see. I think—I think I told her I loved her, then. But I don't know. The memory just... stops as I'm about to say something. I don't know what happened after that. Or if she knows—"

"She knows." I could practically feel the heartache in his words reverberating in my own chest. "Trust me, anyone who has seen you with her, it's crystal clear. Even if you never said it out loud, she knows."

"I used to think the worst part of what happened was that we were taken, experimented on, changed... but I think what hurts the most is knowing that those moments were stolen, too. The most important conversation I *might* have ever had, and I don't know if I'll ever remember what happened after."

He fell silent, the weight of his words settling around us under the night sky. I stared at the wisps of clouds as they ghosted across the face of the moon, and thought back to so many other nights I'd lain under the soft light.

There was something about the cover of night, with only the stars as witness, that brought out these confessions. Words that could only be whispered in the dark, while everyone else was asleep and dreaming. As the space between words grew, I found the courage to speak my own quiet truth.

"I think I'm in love with Dan."

I felt his eyes on me, but I couldn't return his gaze. If I looked up, saw his familiar blue eyes, I didn't think I'd have the courage to keep going.

"And there are times where I could have sworn that maybe he feels something too, but—I'm too scared to say anything. Like if I say the words out loud, it'll break the spell, and everything between us will just disappear like smoke, like it was never there to begin with. And who knows, it could be all in my head—seeing only what I want to see."

Once I opened the door, the words kept coming. Everything I'd talked around for the last few months, finally out in the open.

I took my glasses off, rubbing my tired eyes with the tips of my fingers, taking a deep breath before continuing, "And the part that hurts the most is knowing that what I want is right in front of me, and because I've been too scared to face it, everything might be slipping through my fingers."

"Saying it out loud is the hardest part," Jason said. "No matter who you're actually saying it to."

"No, that's not the hardest part. At least, not anymore."

"What is, then?"

I finally met Jason's eyes, and a pang struck my chest as I spoke the words to him, seeing someone else's crystal blue eyes staring back.

"It's the two of them—together. Dan and Emma."

Jason choked on a breath, sputtering as he replied, "Wait—Dan and *Emma*?" His head whipped around, shooting a look at the place where Dan and Emma slept. "Are you *sure*?"

I hesitated before responding. Because I wasn't sure—and that was another problem.

"No." I sighed. "Sometimes I feel like maybe it's just in my head. But then I see them together, and they've gotten so close. I mean, you see them now. But then lately Emma's been doing this thing where she all but drags me over to hang out with the two of them, and I don't know if it's a soft-launch situation or if she's genuinely just trying to get me and Dan talking again. I have no idea what's been going on and it's confusing as hell."

"I mean, do you want to hear my opinion on it?" Jason asked, tentatively.

"Well, we've come this far, right?" I half joked.

"I know my sister. And everything she's told me about you guys, the Twenty-Somethings, she considers you all to be practically siblings. She doesn't date younger—never has, especially when it comes to men. And with Dan? It's clear she's close with him, especially now. But I can all but guarantee there are nothing but platonic feelings on her side."

"I don't know." I gave him a skeptical look. "They've been practically glued to the hip."

"But you also said she's been trying to pull you into the mix, right?"

I nodded.

"Emma is the most jealous person I have ever met in my life. It's the whole reason I never made a move with Alina before the invasion. Even though she didn't look at Alina that way, Alina was *hers*. Her best friend. If she thought she was being replaced, it would be an all-out war. If Emma had any 'more than friends' feelings at all, she wouldn't let you near him with a ten-foot pole."

He... had a point. And while I had come to almost the same conclusion, it still didn't answer why Dan had been so distant since he and Emma had started getting closer.

"I can't speak for Dan," Jason said, as if reading my mind. "But as far as Emma goes? She cares about you. She wouldn't be trying to intervene if she thought you'd be hurt in the end. Trust me."

And the more I thought about it, the more I believed him.

"I guess I see your point," I said. But instead of feeling relieved, I just felt embarrassed. I'd been moping around like an angsty teenager the last few weeks, and Emma had just been trying to help.

I forced myself to turn around and look in their direction. They were too far away for me to be able to make out their forms, but I knew they were there. The jealousy, the doubt, it was still there, but I was finally starting to see it for what it was. Fear.

Fear of change. Fear of loss. Fear of what would happen if he *did* feel the same.

But Jason was right. The only way to know would be to face the whole thing head-on.

I turned to Jason, and he smiled, grabbing my shoulder with a squeeze.

"I don't know how you do it, man," I said. "Knowing that Carter and Alina are together—being so far from her, feeling everything you do."

"It isn't easy," Jason admitted. "But just like I told Carter before I left, if she cares about him, and if she wants to be with him, I know he'll make her happy. After losing her, that's all I want. I care about both of them. Nothing will ever change that."

"You're like, really well-adjusted."

Jason laughed. "I mean, not going to lie, when I see her again? All bets are off. As much as I love Carter, I'm not just going to back down." A smile curved across his lips as he continued, "I'm going to tell her how I feel. Make this one a memory I actually get to keep. Then, whatever happens after that—we'll just have to leave it up to fate."

Jason's words struck me right in the chest, warming me to my soul.

I wanted him to get his moment. And more than anything, *I* wanted that happiness. For all of us. I'd wasted so much time standing still, falling back into spirals of doubt and past insecurities. But Jason was right. We only had so much time on this planet, and I was tired of wasting it being scared.

I didn't have any control over what happened next, but I could at least make the moments count.

SEPTEMBER 30, 2025

(PART ONE)

We woke up just before sunrise, a tense, excited energy filling the air. Today was the day. We were returning to The Community. And we were going to get our people back.

We talked through our plan one last time, picking it apart and breaking out contingencies for whatever we might face on the journey. Aside from a few pit stops for gas and to let the Octerras hunt, we were driving straight through to the hunting lodge. No breaks for foraging. No breaks for scavenging. No camping out for the night. This was it.

We had no idea what would be waiting for us at the hunting lodge. According to Jason, the resistance had been readying their small force, preparing for a potential emergency evacuation of The Community's many victims. The doctor had been unpredictable, ramping up tests and ordering his guards to carry out punishments for even the smallest of slights. The Community was on the precipice of collapse, its leader past the tipping point of stability. And we were about to be the spark that set the whole powder keg ablaze.

We were just about ready to go, but I had one item on my agenda I needed to take care of before we officially hit the road.

My conversation with Jason from the night before made me realize that I'd been unfairly placing responsibility in Emma's hands for my situation with Dan. And while she might not have known about the thoughts that had been racing through my head the last few weeks, I still felt the need to apologize to her. After all, she'd been trying to help, in her own way.

I spotted her talking with Jason as Gorte stalked around them in a playful circle. As I approached, Gorte launched herself in front of Jason and Emma with a skull-shattering shriek. I fell backward, startled by her sudden attack. My whole body shook and I anticipated the worst as she crept closer.

She lowered on her front legs, baring her teeth in a terrifying grin, her face just inches from mine.

"Gorte! Stop!" Jason yelled, just as Gorte's long black tongue slithered from between her teeth, covering my cheek in a wet, sticky lick.

"Oh my—" I gagged. "What the hell?!" I rubbed at the side of my face with the back of my hand, immediately regretting my decision to approach them with Gorte on the prowl.

"Gortey! We talked about this!" Jason groaned, but Gorte just clicked and chirped merrily in response, trotting away.

Jason jogged over, extending his hand to help me back onto my feet.

"Sorry, Bri. She's just been... excited to finally meet everyone. Even though I've *told her* that humans don't appreciate being *stalked like prey!*" He shot Gorte a look, and I swore, the whuffling sound she made almost sounded like laughter.

"Leave it to you to find the weirdest fucking alien to bond with." Emma rolled her eyes.

She gave me a sympathetic look, using her thumb to wipe off a bit of drool I'd missed as she added, "Damn hell-creature did the same thing to me when I met her."

"Right..." I muttered. "Well at least she doesn't have too much of a taste for human flesh?"

Jason laughed. "So, what's up? You here to round us up to head out?"

"I, uh—" I hesitated, before pushing down my nerves enough to spit out what I'd come here to do. "I actually wanted to talk to Em for a minute, if that's okay? Alone?"

"Oh!" Jason said, surprise crossing his face before he schooled his expression. "I mean, yeah! Totally! I'll just—" He quickly glanced around, before gesturing toward Sander and Gabriela, who were closest to us. "I should check in with Gab and Sander."

He squeezed my shoulder, giving me an encouraging look before jogging over to them. *Way to be subtle, Jayce,* I thought, taking off my glasses and rubbing at the frames as I gathered the courage to say what I had come over to say.

Emma eyed her brother suspiciously before turning her gaze to me. She raised an eyebrow. "So, what's up?"

I took a deep breath, going over the lines I'd practiced on the quick walk over here. "I just wanted to say I'm sorry."

Emma's brows shot up. "Sorry? For what?"

"I know you know things between Dan and I have been weird. And I know you've been trying to help without betraying Dan's trust with whatever he's said to you about it. But after seeing you and Dan together, I don't know, my mind just went wild with all of these assumptions—"

"Whoa, whoa, whoa, slow down!" Emma grabbed my hands. "Brian. First, what do you mean by 'seeing Dan and I together'?" Her bright blue eyes bored into mine as she waited for me to respond.

"Like, last night. You were sleeping with him. You're always together. And he's always, like, holding you, or whispering something to you. And I guess I just jumped to the conclusion that you two were together. Like, *together*."

Emma stared at me for a moment, her confusion quickly turning to frustration as she pulled her hands from mine, taking a step back. "I'm sorry—*what*?"

My heart pounded as my mouth suddenly went dry.

Was Jason wrong? Had I assumed right all along? What the *hell* had I just said?

"Emma, I—" I stammered, but before I could say anything else, she held up her hands, stopping me in my tracks.

"No. Nope. Whatever the fuck you're about to say, Brian, just—no."

"So, there *is* something?"

"No!" she yelled. "God, Brian! Don't you know me better than that? No! What are we, in high school? I would expect this bullshit from the other Twenty-Somethings, but you? *Come on*, dude."

"I'm so confused."

Emma stepped closer and leveled me with a serious look. "I want you to listen very closely when I say this. I don't have *feelings* for Dan. And while I can't tell you everything we talk about, I can fully, completely, one hundred percent reassure you that he *absolutely* does *not* think of me that way, either. And just to make sure I'm clear—there are zero romantic interests between the two of us. None. Nothing. I wouldn't do that to—" She stopped, looking away as she exhaled sharply. When she faced me again her face softened, her voice quieter as she finished, "I wouldn't do that to you."

Heat crept up my neck as I took in her words. So much for preparing for the conversation. I'd still managed to make a mess of it. Thankfully, Emma seemed to understand. I wrapped my arms around her, pulling her in for a hug.

She rested her cheek against my chest, winding her arms around my waist as she murmured, "Brian, after all of the conversations we've had…"

"I'm sorry, Em. I should have just talked to you sooner."

Emma pulled away just enough to look up at me. "No, you should talk to *Dan*. I swear, between the two of you, I am going to lose my mind trying to juggle these conversations."

I laughed, kissing the top of her head before letting go. "Thank goodness Jason came back to talk some sense into me."

"Are you kidding me?!" she screeched. "You talked to *Jason* before talking to *me*? What the fuck, Brian?!"

Jason's laugh echoed from where he stood with Gabriela and Sander, and when I glanced over my shoulder, he was staring back at us, a cheeky grin spread across his face.

"Oh goddamn that asshole and his superhuman hearing," Emma

muttered. "Fuck you, Jason! *I'm* supposed to be the one they confide in!"

From the laughter that followed, it was apparent he wasn't the only one listening in. I looked over my shoulder again, only to find Gabriela was wearing an equally amused grin.

"Of course, the *two* of them are *EAVESDROPPING!*" Emma yelled the last word for emphasis, narrowing her eyes at them as she peered around me.

The laugh that burst from my mouth was filled with a delirious kind of relief. I hadn't realized how much I had been keeping inside, and in just that one conversation, I felt so much lighter. That is, until I caught Emma's eyes again.

A fierce expression took over her face as she practically growled, "I don't care how good his advice is, you were mine first!"

As I laughed in response, a smile cracked her icy exterior, and before long, she was grinning back.

"Thanks, Em. I love you, you know that, right?"

She rolled her eyes, but her voice was filled with warmth as she replied, "I love you too, you dingus. Now let's get ready to hit the road."

We arrived at the hunting lodge later in the afternoon, and by the time we got there, it seemed the party had already started without us. There were clusters of Octerras, with and without Marked Ones in their midst. Some of Cap's and Laurie's contacts had also made the trek down and were working with an older woman with long gray hair who was yelling commands at them like it was her job—which it probably was. There were Marked Ones, kids, and a bunch of other people of all ages milling about the place, and everyone seemed to have a job to do.

Jason directed us to a hunting blind, not too far from the main lodge, where we'd been told to wait until we received further direction. After a while, a white man with a short beard and buzzed hair strolled up.

I knew him.

He was one of the guards who had helped us escape The Community.

He approached Gabriela and Sander with a grin. "I thought we told you two not to come back."

The corner of Sander's mouth tipped into a slight smile. "Well, Kevin, you also told us to get help and to warn whoever we could."

"I'd say we delivered, don't you?" Gabriela added with a shy smile.

"Yeah, you sure as hell did. I can't wait to see the look on Dr. Don's face when we roll up with this crew."

Jason strolled over, nodding a hello to Kevin. "So, you think this is enough to stand a chance?"

"Enough? Jason, this is incredible. We don't just stand a chance—we're going to win this thing," Kevin answered.

"What's the deal at the lodge?" Emma asked, stepping to her brother's side.

"We're setting it up as a kind of refugee station. Guaranteed, more than a few people inside The Community will need medical assistance as soon as we get them out. The doctor has been pumping Marked Ones full of booster serums meant to increase the absorption rates of the alien DNA in their systems. But rather than making Marked Ones stronger, it more often than not has had an opposite effect."

"So, what do we do when we bring them in? Checkups? Fluids? I'm a nurse. Just tell me where I can help and I'm there."

"We'll get you set up with Nan. She's in charge of all of that stuff for us here."

Cap introduced themself next. "I'm Copernicus, but most people call me Cap. I've been communicating with a few of the bushcraft groups that are here—I recognize some of them, but I haven't met all of them face-to-face. If I can help with any kind of coordination, just let me know."

"Thank you," Kevin answered. "Yeah they mentioned you by name when they arrived. You must have been pretty damn convincing to draw them out of hiding. From what some of them have said, they've been holed up in the woods and smaller towns, hoping to wait out the invasion. Well, until you came into contact with them."

"We have some younger people in our group," Michelle jumped in. "I don't want them running into any dangerous situations. Where is the best spot for them to help safely?"

"There are a bunch of kids here. They'll need someone to look over them. I'll be honest, a lot of the people here don't have much experience coordinating rescues like this. But we'll find a role for everyone. For now, just sit tight. We're waiting on word from Marcus, and then we'll know what to do next."

"I still can't believe fuckin' Marcus is the head of this whole damn thing," Sander said, the bitterness evident in his tone. I couldn't blame him. From what he and Gabriela had shared, the man was tough, with a mean streak when challenged.

"Yeah, that was the fucking shocker of a century. Nate and I didn't even know until he drove us out here instead of executing us for treason," Kevin said.

"If you weren't working with Marcus, who were you working with?" Gabriela asked.

"Another guard. Lower in ranks, just enough to slip under the radar. There were a few other regular Community members involved in the resistance, but Nate and I only ever interacted with the one guy. Marcus did a good job of keeping us all separate. Reduced the risk of everyone getting caught if one or two of us accidentally blew our cover."

After sharing a few more logistics, Kevin turned back to Jason. "You're in charge of this group here, and the other Guardians with their riders. Since your Guardian can communicate with the lot of them, she can pass on any orders."

Jason nodded. "We'll be waiting."

As Kevin walked away, Russell let out a low whistle. "Man, this is legit. Jayce, did you know all of these people and 'Terras would be waiting for us here?"

Jason laughed. "I mean, I knew the Octerras were coming, but I had no idea that all of these other people would show up with them. Turns out more Marked Ones have figured out the bond than we could have ever guessed."

No sooner had he finished his sentence, when he froze, his eyes shooting toward a fierce-looking Octerra who was streaking toward us at lightning speed. A look of disbelief crossed his face, just for a moment, before Gorte let out a high-pitched shriek, galloping across the field to meet them as they approached.

"It's her," Jason murmured, staring at the spot where the giant Octerra skidded to a stop, kneeling for the two people atop her back to dismount.

My heart skipped a beat as I recognized her dark wavy hair, her tawny skin, and the grin that lit up her entire face as she hit the ground and immediately started running to Jason.

Alina. She'd gotten out. She was here. And just behind her was Carter, with his signature half-smile.

Jason took off running, and I could barely breathe as Alina leapt into his arms, clinging to him as if he were the only person in the world.

"Guys—" I half whispered, barely able to get the words out. The others were still distracted, checking out the hunting blind and unpacking supplies from the truck. I stayed frozen to the spot, watching the whole scene as Carter jogged over to where Alina and Jason were still entwined.

There was a look in his eyes that I hadn't ever seen before as he studied Jason and Alina. A peaceful kind of calm seemed to pour out of him as he watched the two reunite. Jason looked up at him and there seemed to be some kind of silent exchange, as Carter nodded. The Octerra that had brought them there bumped Jason's arm, and he pressed a palm to her head just briefly before the creature shoved Jason back into Alina. He laughed, hugging Alina tighter, kissing the top of her head.

Emma let out a choked sob, and I finally snapped out of my frozen state as she shoved past me, running toward Alina, Jason, and Carter.

"Lee!" she cried as she threw her arms around Alina, holding on to her as if she were scared Alina would disappear again.

Emma's voice alerted the others, and Sam gasped, yelling out Carter's name.

"They got her out!" Gabriela gasped. And before I knew it, the others were racing toward them, too.

I didn't realize I was crying until a hand squeezed my shoulder, and I quickly pushed my glasses to the side to wipe away the wet trails of tears.

"It's okay, B, they're back. They're safe," Dan murmured. I turned to him, and he gave me a reassuring smile, grabbing my hand, and pulling me toward our friends.

"Brian! Dan!" Carter's face lit up when he saw us, but before we could say anything more, a commotion in the distance pulled our attention away.

Carter cursed under his breath, darting over to where Jason and Alina were speaking urgently, fear coating their expressions.

"Oh shit," Russell exclaimed in a low voice. "It's starting, isn't it?"

"What do we do?" Sam's eyes darted between Cap and where Carter, Jason, and Alina were frantically exchanging words.

Cap rushed over, with Michelle close behind, shouting, "Where do you need us?"

Jason barked out orders. "Anyone with medical experience, even in the slightest, should stay here." He turned to Cap. "That means you, Emma, Michelle, Sam, hell—Gabriela and Sander can be useful, too. Carter, bring them to Nan and Stef. They'll be setting up in the lodge already."

Carter froze, and I didn't miss the fear on his face. I could count on one hand the amount of times I'd seen that look in his eyes, and I knew. We were in trouble.

Dan slipped his hand under mine, lacing our fingers together. My eyes met his, and everything I'd been keeping inside rose to the surface.

"Dan—" I said. But that was all I could get out.

He squeezed my hand, pulling me closer. "Just don't leave my side, okay?"

"Jason, how bad is it?" Carter asked, struggling to keep his voice steady.

Alina answered, her voice barely above a whisper, "It's bad. It's really, really bad."

SEPTEMBER 30, 2025

(PART TWO)

"I NEED SOME HELP OVER HERE!" someone bellowed from outside the lodge.

My head snapped up from the bag of supplies I'd been digging through. It hadn't been long since Carter, Jason, and Alina had left for The Community, but already people were pouring in, reeking of smoke and panic.

"You! Glasses! Go see what they need," the older, gray-haired woman in charge shouted from across the room as she pushed her long strands back under her black bandana. *Nan. Her name is Nan*, I reminded myself.

"On it!" I yelled back, jumping up to see who needed help.

Russell and I had tried to go along with Carter, but Carter had refused to let any of us leave. He had jumped into our truck, speeding away before anyone could argue against the decision, and that had been it.

At least the rest of us were still here—together. But that didn't change the fact that Carter, Alina, and Jason were now lost in the fray, back in the face of the danger that Alina and Carter had just escaped.

"Move faster than that! This is a med ward now," Nan commanded before turning her steely gaze on Emma, ordering her to grab more water bottles and towels.

As I burst outside, I immediately spotted them.

"Please tell me you're the fucking good guys," one of the newcomers called over to me, green eyes wide with panic.

"Ah, yeah! Good guy, reporting for duty."

A younger man was sprawled on the ground, and I cursed under my breath as I rushed over. Judging from the state of *both* of them, they'd been through some kind of hell.

A sinking feeling settled in the pit of my stomach as I took in the man lying at my feet. All color seemed to have drained from his pale face, aside from the yellows and greens of old bruising. Remnants of dried blood coated his dirty clothes, but as I knelt down to quickly scan the rest of him, I didn't see any signs of open wounds.

My eyes traced his sharp jawline down to his neck, and I swallowed hard as I looked for the fluttering of his pulse underneath his skin. Gingerly, I took his wrist. The warmth from his skin pulled a sharp breath of relief from my chest as I registered the faint drum underneath my fingertips. As I measured the beats, my gaze traveled back to his companion.

"What happened?"

"Long story short, we escaped The Community days ago. Or maybe it's been a week? More? Hell, if I know. I've been doing the best I can to take care of him but he's gotten so much worse. Whatever they were injecting us with at The Community, I think it's killing him."

It was then I noticed the faint glow—the tattoos. They were Marked Ones.

"We took a chance and caught a ride with a bunch of people who said help was this way, but as soon as we got close, they dumped us and just took off. What the fuck did we just get dropped into?"

"Well, in the spirit of keeping a long story short, our rescue mission to get people out of The Community just turned into an emergency evacuation. I'm Brian, by the way."

"I'm River. That's James. Please tell me you have someone in there who can help?"

I caught River's worried gaze, and summoned all the confidence I could as I replied, "Lucky for him, you've landed in the right place."

We carried James the rest of the way inside, setting him down on a couch in the quietest part of the lodge we could find. As I slipped my arm out from under him, he finally stirred, a low moan escaping his cracked lips.

"It's okay, buddy. I'm still here," River murmured, brushing sweat-soaked hair from James's forehead.

"Gotta... keep going. Can't be... for nothing," James slurred.

"That's right—we don't stop," River answered, squeezing James's hand.

I looked up just in time to see Emma rushing past, her arms loaded with water bottles and towels.

"Over here!" I called.

Emma's eyes widened as she spotted us.

"What the fuck happened to him?" Her eyes darted between me and River as she set the water bottles and towels on the floor and grabbed James's wrist to check his pulse. "Are you from The Community?"

"Well, yes, but we've been on the run," River answered. "Whatever they did to us in there—this is the result."

"You're abductees?" Emma questioned, her eyes shooting to River.

"In more ways than one—yeah, we're Marked Ones."

Emma's jaw stiffened as she grabbed a towel and bottle of water from the pile, shoving both in my hands as she jumped up, shouting over her shoulder as she ran for the next room, "I'm getting Nan."

I tilted the bottle over a corner of the towel, then handed the bottle to River. Staring down at James, I gently dabbed the towel against the corner of his mouth, trying my best to clean some of the dirt and dried blood from his skin.

Nan rushed over, pushing me out of the way. "Marked Ones. Goddamnit—we need more antiserum!" she yelled.

"Where can I get it?" I asked, unsure what else to do.

I hadn't been around this many injured people since the day the ships had left—when our camp had been attacked. It was getting harder to keep steady. I choked down nausea as the smell of smoke and burnt flesh wafted from the other room. Or maybe it was just in my head. I was having trouble keeping reality and memory separated.

"We don't got anymore antiserum. For now all we can do is keep him comfortable," she said before yelling for Emma. "Red! Make sure he isn't injured anywhere else! I don't like the look of all that dried blood."

As Nan rushed back into the other room, Emma leaned into my side, muttering, "See? This is why I never bothered telling people my real name before Alina found us."

When Emma was taking care of us, when injuries were bad, she always did her best to keep us in a normal headspace. After so many years in the ER, she'd perfected the ability. But I just couldn't pull myself out of my own head.

I turned to her, taking a shuddering breath. I felt like I was about to pass out.

"I don't know if I can go back in that other room."

Understanding spread across her face, and she squeezed my shoulder. "Don't worry. You can stay right here. Consider James your personal charge."

Emma turned to River next. "Listen, River, Brian is going to stay with you two until I get back. I'll check your friend out, but it sounds like we're going to have to wait until we can do more than that. You did a great job getting him here. Now, what about you? Are you okay? Are you hurt?"

"Don't worry about me," River said. "Just do what you can for him. Please. I made a promise to someone and—she risked everything to get us out."

Emma nodded to me, urging me to take over.

"We got this. We'll make sure that promise is kept," I said as convincingly as I could muster.

As Emma rushed out of the room, I struggled to find anything to say to ease River's obvious panic.

"So, you escaped? How did you manage that?" I asked.

"There was this woman. The doctor had the three of us in the gym. He was going to try and force us to bond with a Guardian. Before he could get that far, Alina—"

"Wait—did you just say Alina?" I interrupted, nearly dropping the bottle of water River had just handed back to me.

"Yeah—she got us out. Not just us—there were four others. She sacrificed herself. Made us run while she distracted them."

I couldn't help the proud smile that inched across my face. Of course it had been Alina.

"What's that look?" River questioned, frowning.

"It seems we have a friend in common."

The more time passed, the more nervous I became. I'd been taking care of James as best as I could, with River's help. They'd tracked down some extra clothes, so we were at least able to get James into something clean.

People were coming in at a slower rate now, but there was still no sign of Carter, Jason, or Alina. There were a few other people in the room with River, James, and me—minor burns, cuts, scrapes, nothing serious. Dan, Cap, and Michelle were in here now, and I was thankful to have them working by my side.

A sudden commotion at the front of the lodge drew my attention, and I recognized Alina's voice.

"I have to go back! I can't leave them there!" she yelled frantically.

Cap and Michelle raced into the next room, Dan and I close behind as we took in the sight of her.

She was on her knees, a large box in front of her.

Michelle rushed to her side, cupping Alina's sobbing face in her hands. "Alina, honey, look at me. What happened?"

Alina gasped for breath, shoving the box forward as she tried to scramble to her feet. "The viles—the antiserums are in there. I can't —I have to go—Jason and Carter—"

"No, no, no—you aren't going anywhere. Not like that," Nan's voice cut through the chaos. A small crowd of onlookers were forming and Nan shooed them away. "You hurt? What happened?"

"He made me go! He made Anat take me back, but the doctor— the invader—Marcus is dead."

"Wait—invader? What do you mean, invader?" Dan asked, as we both rushed to her side.

I slid an arm around her waist, bracing her against my body to try and help her stay on her feet. Her tattoo was so bright, I could hardly look at it without squinting. She was more than panicked—terror consumed her. Dan braced her other side, helping me walk her over to a chair.

"He said they never left. That they were still here—watching—"

But before she could say anything else, something heavy slammed into the doorframe.

An Octerra screeched, and Alina's eyes darted to the door. "Jason! Carter!" she yelled.

"Someone, help!" Carter's voice thundered as he hovered in the doorway, his arms wrapped around Jason. They were both covered in blood. "Please! You have to help him!"

"No—" Alina's voice broke.

Dan and I rushed to the door where Carter was struggling to support Jason's weight.

There was so, so much blood.

"Are you hurt?!" I managed to choke out.

Carter shook his head. "I'm fine—focus on Jason!"

Just outside, Gorte let out a pained screech, practically howling as she paced outside. As soon as Carter and Jason cleared the entry, she rammed her body against the doorway again, clawing at the frame, trying to push her way in.

"Bring him over here!" Nan yelled. "And someone get that damn Guardian out of here! She'll tear the entire place down! Where's my nurse? Red!"

"No!" Dan shot back. "You can't bring Red in here!"

"And why the fuck not? I need another pair of hands!"

"He's her brother," I whispered.

Nan's eyes widened, and she cursed under her breath as she cut Jason's shirt open, trying to find the source of his bleeding.

Alina clung to Jason's hand, begging, "Stay with me! Please, stay with me. Please don't leave me. I can't lose you now. I just got you back."

I backed away from the table, nearly slipping in the blood that trailed from the doorway to where Jason lay too still on the table.

"I'm so sorry," Nan said, her tone far too gentle, too calm for what was happening. "I'm so sorry, there isn't anything we can do."

"No. No! There has to be something. You have to help him!" Carter exploded.

A low whine echoed from the door, and my eyes shot to the spot where Gorte had wedged herself in the frame. She slowly pulled back from the battered doorway, letting out another mournful howl before turning and bounding for the tree line. And before Nan could say another word, I knew.

We all knew.

He was gone.

OCTOBER 3, 2025

Days had passed, and we were nowhere near recovered.

The fight was far from over. Especially with the confirmation that the invaders were still lurking around somewhere.

A recon group had gone back to The Community in search of the invader that Alina and Carter had seen with Dr. Don at the end. But all they found was the doctor's body lying next to Marcus's torn-up remains. The only evidence that there had been anything else there was a trail of black viscous fluid leading away from the scene. At least Carter's shot had injured the damn thing.

The days following were quiet.

We took care of the wounded. Did what we could to help those who needed it. I kept myself distracted by learning whatever first-aid I could from Nan, and helping River take care of James, who was still recovering. With Emma out of commission, we needed more knowledgeable hands to help care for the injured. I knew, at least in this way, I could help. So I did.

We had enough antiserum to treat most of the Marked Ones who'd shown up in critical condition, and it seemed that they all were starting to heal. Once the antiserum took effect, the results were quick. Turns out, one of the doctor's assistants was also part of the resistance, and she'd been working on the antiserum with the excuse that they might need it as a "do-over" in case the Sovereign experienced the side effects so many Marked Ones had succumbed to. Apparently being "chosen" didn't apply to those willing to take power in whatever form they believed they deserved.

I was doing my best to find the bright spots, but more often than not, the cold, dark well of heartache seemed to win. The pain of loss had no end, embedded like shrapnel. And as time wore on, it only seemed to dig in deeper.

I wandered the edge of the tree line, listening for the Octerras. Most of them had taken to the denser parts of the hunting range, opting for the cover of trees. According to Gabriela, the creatures were on high alert, looking out for any signs of the invaders.

I sat against the base of a tree, hugging my knees to my chest. Grief came in waves, and today I just couldn't stop myself from being pulled under the tide.

My mind often wandered back to the day Jason had come back to us. The way he and Gorte had burst into the clearing. The way his smile had lit up when he'd seen us, and how he'd sat with me that night when my mind had been spiraling. I hadn't known Jason long, but that day he'd turned the corner from being a casual acquaintance in our group to being a true friend. I hated that I had never gotten to thank him for that.

I felt guilty for wallowing in my own sorrow when Emma, Alina, and Carter were devastated beyond measure. I hadn't realized just how close Carter and Jason had gotten in the weeks they'd spent together, but seeing what losing Jayce had done to him was confirmation enough. I tried to be stronger around them, but I could only push my own feelings down so far before everything bubbled right back up to the surface.

Here, alone, with no one else around, I could finally let myself break.

My shoulders heaved as all of the emotions I'd kept pent up overflowed. I dug my fingers into my knees, pulling them tighter against me as heavy sobs shook my body.

I couldn't keep doing this—finding hope, only to have it torn away. Seeing my friends hurting so deeply. So, so much heartbreak. No matter what we did, how hard we fought against it, pain and loss always seemed to win in the end.

How could we ever move on from this, knowing that we would only have to face more danger, death, and destruction? When would it end?

I didn't hear his approach, but as strong arms wrapped around my shoulders I knew it was him. And instead of fading deeper into the hole that threatened to swallow me, I let myself fall into his familiar embrace.

"I'm here. I got you. I'm here, B," Dan murmured, the warmth of his breath hitting my neck as he tried to comfort me.

My arms wound around his waist, holding on to him like a lifeline as his hand moved to the back of my neck, anchoring me against him. I let myself sink into him, holding on tighter than I had ever allowed myself before.

"It's not fair." Shuddering breaths broke through my tears, leaving the numb, throbbing ache of loss in its place. "It's not fucking fair."

"I know," he whispered against my skin, hugging me closer—so close I knew he had to feel my heart pounding.

His cheek brushed against mine, damp with his own tears, as he pulled back just enough to see my face. A worry line carved deeper across his forehead as his deep brown eyes studied mine. We stayed like that for an extended breath, so many unspoken words between us, I didn't know where to start.

Dan broke the silence first.

"Bri... I'm sorry." His thumb absently trailed along the pulse point in my neck where his hand was still clasped. "I haven't been around, and I know you've noticed. Whenever things get too much, I cut myself off. Find a distraction. Create distance. I always have. And you don't deserve it. I just—I don't know how to do this."

He paused, breaking eye contact as he closed his eyes, taking a deep breath.

My heart sank. I knew where this conversation was headed. I'd been here before. Nausea churned in my stomach, and I forced myself to choke out, "It's okay. You don't have to say anything else. I get it. You don't have to stay."

His eyes blinked open as his brow furrowed. "I don't have to—what?"

"Really. It'll just hurt more if—"

"Wait, what do you think is happening right now?"

"That you're done. That I'm trying too hard and it's too much. That you don't want—"

His eyes widened and he let out a sharp exhale. "Is that what you think?"

"What am I supposed to think?" I replied, beyond exhausted from the back-and-forth, the pushing, pulling, and letting go.

Dan didn't respond, not at first. He just stayed there, staring back at me with an expression I couldn't translate. And even still I was captivated, lost in his gaze.

His eyes lowered as he pulled me in closer, resting his forehead against mine. His breath hit my lips as he murmured, "For once, Bri, please just don't think."

The touch was so soft, I thought I'd imagined it at first. But as I felt the brush of his lips, parting ever so slightly, I gave in. I pressed my lips to his, and everything else faded away.

My fists tightened against the fabric of his shirt as he pulled me in, kissing me back. A shiver rolled down my spine as months of questioning whether this was all one-sided melted away in the heat of the moment.

With Dan's hand still firmly gripping the back of my neck, he wrapped his other arm tighter around me, pulling me even closer against him. His chest pressed into mine as I ran my hands along the planes of his back, barely able to comprehend that this was actually happening. His lips curved into a smile as he kissed me, pushing me back into the grass until there was no place our bodies weren't connected.

I cupped his jaw in one hand as the other pressed against his chest, tracing up to the curve of his clavicle, the dip of his shoulder.

"I'm sorry I waited so long," he whispered against my mouth.

I stared up at him, breathing heavily. I didn't want to question it—didn't want to stop. But I couldn't help myself. I had to know.

"So, why now?"

He paused, his lips just a breath away as his eyes burned into mine. "I was scared. I've never felt this way about anyone before. When Alina was taken, seeing how it wrecked Carter and J—" He paused, squeezing his eyes shut as he took a breath, steadying himself. "I saw what losing her did to them. And I knew that if I let myself fall deeper... I couldn't risk that kind of pain. So, I tried to be there for Emma, instead. I thought that if I focused on helping her, maybe I could distract myself enough to let it fade away. But that didn't work, either."

"Well, thank goodness for that," I joked half-heartedly.

He kissed me again, once, twice, before replying with a tilted smile, "Yeah, thank goodness for that."

"And you're sure you want this?"

Dan nodded. "I'm sure. Because whatever happens next, I don't want to face it without you. Without us."

"Us?"

A rare soft smile crept across Dan's face as he gently kissed me again, cupping my jaw. "Yeah. Us. I love you, B."

I didn't hesitate before crashing my lips against his again, pulling him closer to me. He kissed me harder and his hand fell to the column of my neck. As his lips kissed a searing line against my jaw, I stammered, "So, just to clarify, when you said you love me, you didn't mean like, just as a friend?"

Dan paused, the corner of his mouth quirking up like he'd been waiting for the question.

"Definitely not just as a friend."

"Okay, good. Because you're still my best friend, but I've definitely been in love with you for, like, way longer than I should probably admit. Like—cinematic, epic ballad kind of love."

Dan laughed quietly, resting his forehead against mine. "I can relate."

"I love you, Dan."

He pressed his lips against mine, kissing me slowly, lingering against my touch, before breaking apart just long enough to reply, "I love you, too."

And it was more than enough to finally quiet my mind.

As we made our way back to our camp, Dan kept his arm around me, holding me close. Now that all of our barriers were down, I never wanted to let go. And thankfully, Dan didn't seem to want to, either.

Emma looked up as we approached, and when she saw the way we were connected, a smile curved across her lips—the first one in days. "Well, it's about damn time," she said.

Her words caught the attention of the rest of our group, and Sam let out a little squeal, jabbing her elbow into Russell's side. "It's happening!" she whispered.

"Ow! What's happening?" Russell asked, rubbing his ribs, before glancing over at Dan and me. His eyes widened as he exclaimed, "Oh shit! Is this a hard launch?"

Dan rolled his eyes, but the corner of his mouth curved into a smile as he looked at me. His gaze darted to my lips before he reached up, tilting my chin toward him, murmuring, "What do you say? Hard launch?"

I nodded, not hesitating for even a fraction of a second before I kissed him in front of everyone.

Because no matter what was waiting for us tomorrow, the next day, or the day after that—this moment was ours.

More than that—mine.

There were still grief, loss, fear, uncertainty, sorrow, and hardships yet to come. That much was for sure, and nothing would erase the devastation we'd experienced. But I was beginning to realize that while pain was inevitable, it didn't always mean defeat. And I wanted to believe in a future where we came out on the other side stronger for the battles we'd faced.

One day, history books would tell the story of how the human race had fought against the alien invaders that had threatened to destroy humanity. But between the lines, there would always be a deeper story to be told. One where love was still stronger than the forces that had set out to destroy us. A story where sacrifice and risking it all led to a chance for happiness.

A new beginning, ready to unfold.

THANK YOU!

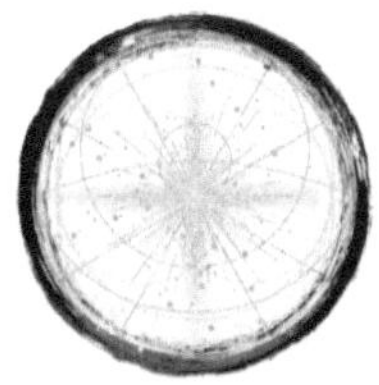

Thank you for reading the Afterglow Rising Novella:
Between the Lines
Don't forget to leave a star rating and written review on Amazon
and/or GoodReads!

GoodReads   Amazon

ACKNOWLEDGMENTS

I hope you enjoyed Brian's point of view, and that the love story at the heart of this novella got you in all the right feels! These characters mean so, SO much to me, and every time I get to share them with you, it makes my heart that much happier.

Now—a few thank yous in order!

First, Loren Lee, thank you for being the first pair of eyes to read **Between the Lines.** Your feedback, encouragement, and support mean more than you could ever know. And thank you for always picking up the phone 🖤

My Stace Invaders—Shelby, Sam, Margaret, Alex, and Bee, thank you for being so ride or die for this series. All of the support you've shown **Afterglow** MAKES MY LIFE.

To my family—Mike, E, L, and MOMMMMMM, you are the best hype people, and I LOVE YOU!!!

And thank you to my friends, Jenna, Suzanne, Lauren, and Caroline for all of your real-time reactions. You're where **Afterglow** began, and I love you forever for being such an integral part of this wild journey.

To my editor, Sam—thank you for believing in me, encouraging me, and for all of your comments and feedback. Thank you for letting me keep so many em dashes, and for all of your advice. I am so lucky to work with you!

And to you, my wonderful reader—without you, truly, none of this would be possible. Your support helps me to continue on this journey, and I appreciate every kind word, unhinged message, and show of support you throw my way.

Book three, the final chapter of the **Afterglow Rising Trilogy** is set to release in late spring of 2026, and I cannot wait for you to see how it all ends. Be sure to sign up for my newsletter and follow me on social media for all the latest updates!

See you later, space invader.

🖤 -Stacey LP

SIGN UP FOR STACEY'S NEWSLETTER!

To stay up to date on all upcoming releases, sneak peeks, giveaways, event announcements, and more, don't forget to sign up for Stacey LP's newsletter!
Please scan the below QR code, or visit:
www.authorstaceylp.com
to sign up!

ABOUT THE AUTHOR

Stacey LP was born and raised on Long Island in NY, and currently resides in Texas.

After a major plot twist where she lost her full-time job of almost a decade in a mass layoff, Stacey's friends urged her to pursue her dream of writing a book of her own...and thus, an author was born.

Stacey writes in the sci-fi and fantasy genres, frequently weaving love stories into each plot. When she isn't writing (or reading), Stacey enjoys spending time with her husband, children, two cats, and goofball of a dog...or going to pop punk shows. #elderemo4ever

Stacey has an MA in English Literature from SUNY New Paltz and is proud (aka relieved) to finally use her degree for more than just a punchline.

You can find Stacey on Instagram, Tik Tok, and Threads at:
    @authorstaceylp

ALSO BY STACEY LP

AFTERGLOW RISING TRILOGY:

Afterglow Rising From the Ashes

Afterglow Defiance Ignited

Between the Lines: An Afterglow Rising Novella

ANTHOLOGY:

Dark Fairytales For the Unloved (Vol I) an Indie Author Collective

Stay up to date by following Stacey on GoodReads and Amazon.

GoodReads

Amazon

www.ingramcontent.com/pod-product-compliance
Lightning Source LLC
Chambersburg PA
CBHW031408310726
48971CB00003B/788